10,000 Gallo

Mark Woodward

Copyright © 2020 by Mark Woodward

All rights reserved.

No part of this publication may be reproduced, distributed, or transmitted in any form or by any means, including photocopying, recording, or other electronic or mechanical methods, without the prior written permission of the publisher, except in the case of brief quotations embodied in critical reviews and certain other non-commercial uses permitted by copyright law. For permission requests, contact the publisher.

Mind The Cat Publishing

info@mindthecat.uk

ISBN: 978-1-9163670-0-5

Dedication

This book is dedicated to the peoples of China, whose nation provided a welcoming and safe refuge for those fleeing persecution in the early 20th century.

About the Author

Mark Woodward grew up and went to school in Bristol. He studied archaeology and anthropology at university and holds an MBA from Kingston University. He worked for a merchant bank in the City of London and subsequently created and ran a forensic science based technology company. Mark is heavily involved in environmental issues and challenges facing bees and other pollinators. This is his first book.

Acknowledgement

Thank you to my family and friends who encouraged me to write this book. It was a labour of love, and I am so appreciative of all the support and love that you extended to me!

Preface

In the early 20th Century, tens of thousands of Russian Jews found a new home in Harbin, Manchuria, bringing their culture and western classical music. The Harbin Symphony Orchestra founded in 1908 is the oldest symphony orchestra in China and the Harbin No.1 Music School founded in 1928 was the first music school in China. The musical tradition continues and in 2010, Harbin was recognised by UNESCO as 'The Music City'

To many in the West, it will be a surprise that China was already fighting WW2 when hostilities in Europe broke out. The brutal Japanese occupation of Manchuria from 1931 escalated in 1937 to a full-scale conflict at Lugouqiao (known as the Marco Polo Bridge incident). Contrary to popular belief, despite an estimated 15 to 20 million dead and an astonishing 90+ million Chinese becoming refugees, the resilient Chinese neither surrendered nor were completely defeated.

The Chinese suffered brutality not only at the hands of the Japanese occupying army but also from their own Chiang Kai-Shek, the nationalist leader of the Kuomintang party who had ordered the destruction of the dykes on the Yellow River in an attempt to stop a Japanese advance. The breach caused 500,000 Chinese deaths and made 4.5 million homeless. The title of this book is taken from a contemporary description where the sound of the water escaping was likened to the sound of 10,000 galloping horses.

My own experience of travelling in China has been full of kindness, politeness and culture. It is that background that prompted me to write this manuscript, based on true episodes in the 20th Century and the Superpower that China has become today.

Contents

Dedication .... *i*
About the Author .... *ii*
Acknowledgment .... *iii*
Preface .... *iv*

Chapter 1 .... *1*
Reunited ....
Chapter 2 .... *18*
From Russia with Love ....
Chapter 3 .... *36*
Catching Up ....
Chapter 4 .... *53*
Invasion ....
Chapter 5 .... *71*
An Old Friend ....
Chapter 6 .... *89*
Marco Polo ....
Chapter 7 .... *107*
Demons ....
Chapter 8 .... *125*
Safety Zone ....
Chapter 9 .... *144*
Guilt Of The Past ....
Chapter 10 .... *162*
Fight Or Flight ....
Chapter 11 .... *181*
A Life of Strife ....
Chapter 12 .... *201*
Letting Go ....

Chapter 13 219
Long Way Around ....
Chapter 14 241
The First Song..
Chapter 15 259
Season of Migration..
Chapter 16 282
The Final Goodbye ....

Page Left Blank Intentionally

Chapter 1
Reunited

Leaning his elbows heavily on the bar, Elias narrowed his eyes and peered deeply into the ice-cold tumbler that contained the second drink he'd ordered tonight. It was his usual: the Old Fashioned. He picked it up in his right hand and swirled the dark liquid around, all the while gazing into it as though willing it to reveal the future or illuminate his past to him.

He felt inebriated, although he knew he wasn't. Purposefully, he put the rim of the glass to his mouth and downed the drink all at once. The liquor burned his throat as it went down and left a slightly sweet and bitter taste in his mouth, exactly the way he liked it. He gestured to the bartender for a refill and then turned his head around to examine his surroundings.

The gas chandeliers on the ceiling lit up the setting, albeit dimly. Brightness overlaid with shadow was draped like a quilt over the interior of the bar, revealing some spots and obscuring some; the interplay between darkness and light only enhanced the deliberately maintained atmosphere of secrecy. It seemed like the perfect place to exchange confidences – a place where you'd rather whisper than talk out loud, because to do otherwise might be akin to breaching an unspoken code of conduct. Most of the walls were upholstered in red leather. On one side where there was a round arch, several heads of stuffed animals hunted down over the years were mounted triumphantly. Maybe it was the character of Washington DC with its sly political manoeuvrings and stealthy dealings where the bar was located that lent it this air of ambiguity.

Elias saw that there were barely any other people in the bar. He lit a cigarette and took a long puff. Releasing the smoke through his nose, he picked up the glass that the bartender had placed in front of him, his third drink for the night. He sipped at it, feeling detached from everything. He was in a curious mood, unwilling to listen to his own better judgment. So he smoked and drank, perhaps to calm down his nerves which, for some reason, were especially frayed tonight. He knew he should pay heed to his limousine driver's warning who had told him to not drink too much, not tonight, for he had an important event to attend in a matter of a few hours. It was a government affair and Elias, an acclaimed professional violinist, wasn't particularly looking forward to it. He wasn't very excited for the night, even though he had been specially invited or rather summoned to welcome the Chinese delegation led by a senior Chinese official, to Washington. Though he was a celebrated violinist, he felt that in this instance, he was invited more for his acquaintance with the Chinese tradition than for his musical gift.

Though he had lived in America for many years now, as a child he'd spent time in Harbin, China for a few years. That was enough time for him to become fluent in Mandarin – one would be surprised at the rapid speed with which children learn a language – and gain an insider's understanding of the Chinese way of life. The ceremony was in honour of the delegation from China that was visiting Washington DC after President Nixon's historic trip to China last year.

He assumed that it would be a stiff and formal ceremony, in line with the only now thawing relationship between the two countries. Setting aside longstanding differences or brought together by mutual distrust of the Soviet Union, the two countries were making headway towards building a friendlier relationship. This signalled a shift in the international political arena. Now the two countries had decided to open offices in Beijing and Washington to open dialogue and liaise officially. Elias recalled the President's visit from last year quite clearly even though he had tried to avoid following it too closely; he did that simply because he felt that he no longer had any personal stakes in that part of the world which had left him only with rusty reminiscences. The time that he had spent in China was shrouded with cobwebs in his memory – he had never really tried to dust them off for he was afraid of reopening old wounds that had never really healed.

Even so, he'd read newspapers that had ardently covered the official visit. The press was too excited to report every bit of the news that they could get their hands on, obviously. The front pages of the newspapers were splashed with such screaming headlines as *"NIXON ARRIVES IN PEKING TO BEGIN AN 8-DAY VISIT; MET BY CHOU AT AIRPORT"* and *"NIXON AND MAO HOLD SURPRISE HOUR-LONG TALK"* and *"NIXON STARTS 'JOURNEY FOR PEACE'"* and *"GET TO KNOW THE U.S. BETTER, NIXON URGES"*. And then there was the news on television, which reported the same events but with ten times the sense of urgency. The events or maybe the reporting of those events – made Elias feel as though the two countries were on the brink of something monumental. He'd watched as the scenes on the television screen showed President Nixon being met at the airport by the Chinese officials. He'd seen the stills of him shaking hands with Mao Zedong as the First Lady stood smiling in a red dress.

He could still recall the close-ups of the side profile of the two men: Nixon as the taller one with a hooked nose, sagging jowls and thick brows and Mao as shorter, with a round face, snub nose and a diving widow's peak. He recalled images of Nixon and the Chinese Premier Zhou Enlai seated on sofas, presumably engrossed in a discussion, with the former pointing the forefingers of both his hands up, as though to symbolize his hopes for the future trajectory of US-Sino relationship as the latter stared into the camera.

He'd watched President Nixon toasting Zhou Enlai, and he had seen as the two had dinner and drinks for the entire world to witness. The media frenzy was intense and invasive. There was no place where Elias was spared from the news, and its accompanying images. He felt transported to China all over again and without his express will. Now, an important Chinese official was visiting his adopted country, America. And like a good host, he was to be there to welcome him warmly. He was expected to play the soulful music he was known for to entertain the officer. And considering the authorities through research of his background, Elias also expected that he would be required to speak to him in his language, Mandarin, so as to allay any feelings of homesickness that might ail him. These were all his inferences. The truth was, he didn't really mind all this. He was a musician and playing for an audience was part of it. Only tonight, a faint, unsought mist of melancholy had settled on him.

He chalked it up to his artistic temperament, but knew deep in his heart that he was bothered because this event had stirred the memories of his past. Now, image after image from his childhood was intruding on his conscious mind – this is what he had kept all locked up so tightly that it had never seen the light of day. He was still holding the pictures back; he knew that if he let it, the past would flood his present and drown him in the pain that he had learned to soothe over the years.

Memory functioned on the powers of association, and it was so unpredictable that he could never foretell what would cause a spark and set fire to the straw house that housed his memories. It wasn't that he avoided or denied his past – only that he never indulged in reliving it because to do so would cause him distress that he would rather avoid.

Even so, his mind was involuntarily transported to his time in Harbin, China. He could still vividly recall the place where he lived when he was a child. The buildings, the streets, the air, and the people. He was so young back then, that time had seemed to progress at the pace of a snail.

That is why he could never understand when some of the elderly women around him used to sit together, shake their heads and say in voices that sounded as wrinkled as their faces, *"Guāng yīn sì jiàn!"*[1] It was only now when he looked back that he could somewhat understand what they meant. The older he got, the faster time seemed to pass. But even though this past appeared to be distant and remote, he knew he could still bid it to come alive – only, he never did so, at

---

[1] Time flies like an arrow.

least not willingly. Right now, as he sat comfortably ensconced in his chair in the warm surroundings of the bar, his mind rebelliously conjured up the past for him. The bitter winters of his childhood in Harbin replaced the cosy atmosphere of the bar; he could almost feel the cold that bit through his skin to his bones. He could visualise the Saint Sophia Cathedral, with its round dome with green tips, which stood at the corner of Toulon Street.

That building, his parents said, always reminded them of their home country because of its Neo-Baroque architecture. He could still recall the wild laughter of his friends as he ran with them on the Jihong Bridge, playful and carefree as the horse-drawn carriages passed them by. And if he closed his eyes and listened very closely, he knew he would hear the trace of the soft notes of music that floated from the symphony orchestra which trained young musicians in the art of music.

Elias closed his eyes and shook his head to bring himself back to the present. His limousine driver who was to escort him to the venue was standing by his side, waiting for him with a barely concealed frown of disapproval on his face. He reluctantly got up, knowing he had to respond to the call of duty. Shaking his dim mood off, he briskly walked to the car near the curb. He got into the limousine and once seated, stretched out his legs to get comfortable. The driver started up the engine and began driving to the location he had been informed of. Elias watched the swiftly changing scenes through the glass screen of the window. It all seemed as fleeting as a dream. A phrase from the past came drifting up through his memories, like a fallen golden leaf of autumn, *"Niǎoér chànggē bùshì yīnwéi tāmen yǒu le dáàn, érshì yīnwéi tāmen yǒu gē yào chàng."*

It meant, *'A bird does not sing because it has an answer. It sings because it has a song.'* Elias too, had a song. He had his violin and he knew he was going to play it for the Chinese official who had come to visit America. The violin case was resting on the seat beside him. He ran his hands over its smooth surface, caressing it with affection as well as gratitude. The violin had saved him. He felt it was an extension of his body. It was like his arm or his finger, he could no more imagine a life without it as he could without his essential limbs. The love of music that he had was strong enough to somewhat put him in a better frame of mind. He was a performer and he would perform in the best way that he knew. Clasping his hands together, he prepared himself mentally for the performance to come, believing that it would go well. The car stopped near the front steps of the building. Elias stepped out and began to walk towards the large hall, taking long, determined strides. The driver followed him, carrying his violin case; he embraced it closely, as though it were a fragile child that needed protection.

Once at the door, Elias was led by the staff there to a waiting room. He remained there until the Chinese guests arrived a few minutes later. The ceremony scheduled for the night had begun. Walking up to the main hall, Elias almost immediately spotted the Chinese delegation and the important official who was wearing a dark-coloured suit. He was of slight stature.

His hair was grey and he had wide cheekbones. His face seemed as smooth as a baby's skin, and his nose seemed too small for it. Elias remembered the greeting etiquettes from his childhood and waited till he was directed to approach and welcome the man. Two males, who seemed like government officials to him, accompanied him to the group with which the Chinese official, his name was Zhao Jiangsu, was standing. As Elias got near to them, they politely broke off their conversation and turned to greet him. Elias gave a deep bow and waited for one of the government officials to introduce him. He knew that manners dictated that he be introduced first, since he was the younger of the two. When the official was done introducing him, Elias gave a deep bow to Zhao Jiangsu, clasping his hands together to give him a traditional fist and palm salute, and then said, *"Ni hao! Wo de ming zi shi Elias."*[2] The older man looked at him with a sparkle in his eyes, as though he was very pleased to see him. He extended his hand to Elias which he took and shook warmly.

Something about this man seemed slightly, indescribably familiar to him and Elias felt good to be in his presence. They casually talked for a while. Elias easily slipped into Mandarin as he talked, the language resurfacing effortlessly even though he hadn't really used it in a long time. He was still fluent in it and could hold a conversation like a native Chinese. He asked polite questions regarding Zhao Jiangsu's trip, then talked about the weather, the time change and the

---

[2] Hello! My name is Elias.

resultant jetlag. Zhao Jiangsu earnestly answered his questions but seemed to be withholding any questions of his own. He told Elias that he was looking forward to watching him play the violin again. The 'again' caught Elias a bit by surprise but he assumed it to be a mistake. Soon, it was time for him to head up to the small platform that had been set up for him.

He walked up to the dais and stood in the middle. He knew all eyes were drawn to him even though he wasn't looking at them just now. He had all his focus on his instrument; in the present moment, he was lost to all else. He picked it up and held it in his hands before resting it against his left shoulder. The left side of his jaw rested against the chinrest of the violin. Holding it firmly, he lifted up the freshly-tightened bow in his right hand.

Then he checked the strings and tuned them a bit. In position, he took a deep breath and finally began to play. Instantly, ripples of poignant music soared over the hall, enveloping all the attendants in its sweet melancholy. The melody that Elias was playing was classical music; he was a trained classical musician. The music started out slowly and gently, like waves lapping against the shore on a quiet sundrenched afternoon. It was unhurried leisure basking in its own beauty. Then all of a sudden, the violin produced a sharp, high-pitched trill, as though to signal an abrupt, painful change. It was not jarring to the senses, though, and only felt like a natural progression of the passionate story that Elias was narrating through his music. The notes seemed alarmed and hurried. If visualised, it would probably look like people trapped in a sinking ship fighting to stay alive.

The audience held their breath, waiting for the denouement. Slowly, deliberately the notes became calm again. They transitioned back to a graceful, elegant tune reminding Zhao Jiangsu of the day's end when the sun goes down and the birds glide over the sky to vanish into the horizon. The performance ended then. Everyone, including Zhao Jiangsu, broke instinctively into a round of applause.

The performance had spoken to all of them differently. To Zhao Jiangsu, it seemed to tell a story of incredible joys and heartbreaking sorrows. It simply seemed to him like life: profound, surprising, and made richer by the interplay of brightness and gloom. He couldn't help but feel a twinge of unnamed regret which he did nothing to assuage. He watched the young music maestro with pride in his eyes, happy to see the talent he had been appreciated as it deserved. He got up on his feet as Elias came down the stage. He saw as Elias shook the hands of a few people who had come up to him to congratulate him on his impressive performance. He saw him acknowledge them politely, with a smile on his face that didn't really reach his eyes.

In a while, Elias noticed that Zhao Jiangsu was waiting for him. He looked in his direction and started walking his way. Seeing Elias approach, Zhao Jiangsu's face lit up and a bright, paternal smile softened it. It creased his face and caused his eyes to close into half-moons that instantly made him look younger than he really was. Elias saw the smile and was stricken with a sense of déjà vu: he felt as if he had seen the same smile before, maybe in his past life.

He couldn't really place the older man, though, and didn't think much about it anyhow. He could have seen a similar face anywhere in his past. His thoughts were still occupied by his performance which he felt went well, satisfying him and pleasing his audience. He was a perfectionist when it came to his art, and could catch his audience's discontent as though he had special sensors to gauge their reaction, even that which wasn't explicitly expressed. He just knew when his listeners left his performance feeling that they had had the experience of a lifetime. He had poured out his heart in the performance. The long, tormented sobs of the violin and its prolonged, exultant cries, and everything that came in between those two emotions were crafted to tell a tale. Elias felt that he had successfully expressed to his audience what he had wanted to communicate to them.

He had told a story and they had listened. And he'd always felt that listening was the best and the most generous gift that anyone could ever bestow on others. The remnants of the despair that had enveloped him earlier began to clear away. He felt seen, he felt heard. Even without the praise that he had received from the people, those two things alone were enough to make him happy.

He got near Zhao Jiangsu and smiled in response to his smile, which really was infectious. The older man showered praise on him which Elias could tell was not only sincere but also proud. Elias felt that Zhao Jiangsu was not just moved by his art but had felt it very personally and understood it better than anyone else in attendance. It was as though the music Elias had played was a secret code between the two men, or a language which only the two of them in this vast hall were fluent in. Elias was again perturbed by the feelings of familiarity and strangeness that came over him together. He didn't know what it was but it really was something that he could not deny. Then, without warning, Zhao Jiangsu reached out his arms and pulled Elias into a close embrace. To say that Elias was taken aback would be an understatement. Caught by surprise, he didn't resist and just returned the hug, learning down automatically.

Zhao Jiangsu let him go then and whispered in a voice raw with regret, *"Do you really not remember me, Elias?"* Elias didn't know what to say. As he stared into the older man's face, trying to read it like the cypher it had suddenly become, the pieces of the puzzle that had perplexed him since he had met Zhao Jiangsu started to fall into place.

As though by magic, the wrinkles on the older man's face and the lines at the corners of his eyes and mouth disappeared; before Elias's eyes appeared a face smooth and young. The hair, too, was no longer grey but black. The man before Elias had suddenly transformed from a stranger into someone he had known long, long ago.

"*Jiangsu tài!*" Elias exclaimed. Recognition had finally dawned on him. He finally saw that the man before him, the Chinese official who had travelled all the way from China, was someone that he owed his life to. He saw tears come into Zhao Jiangsu's eyes which, now that Elias noticed them, looked older but still very familiar. They were still full of unnamed sorrow, just as Elias had always seen them.

When Elias had last seen this man, he was young and Elias was a child. He didn't know such emotions then or if he did, he didn't know their names. But now, Elias was aware of what Zhao Jiangsu's eyes said of what they had been saying, probably since the time of the war. For the first time, Elias felt that he had really and truly seen the man who was the reason why he was alive today.

Chapter 2
From Russia with Love

The year was 1930. Mikhail Abrams hummed as he walked on Zhongyang Dajie[3], sometimes also called the Kitaiskaya Ulitsa (Chinese Street), in his adopted city of Harbin, China. The street ran all the way from Jingwei Jie up to the Sōnghuā River and Mikhail liked walking along it; if the weather allowed.

At present, it was July and the climate was moderate enough for him to take a walk through the city centre; otherwise, the low temperatures in the city meant that he had to make his way home from his store as quickly as he could to avoid the bitingly cold winds.

His own clothes store was situated on this street which stretched over 1400 metres; it was right across from the famous Daoliquilin Shop that was established in 1919. It was Mikhail's ambition to make his shop as famous as that one.

---

[3] Central Street

Though getting his business up and running after he immigrated to Harbin from Russia with his young family in tow was an uphill task, he was pleased to say that he was doing well for himself and his family now. The cobblestoned main street was busy at this time of the day. As he strolled homeward, he heard the steady thrum of carriage wheels and the endless buzz of the pedestrians on the road; he felt that he was a small but integral part of the hustle and bustle of Harbin.

From where he was walking, he saw the emerald green dome of the Saint Sofia Church rising up in the sky. The sight gave him a sense of comfort and a sense of belonging; he was a Russian Jew in China and after having escaped his home country, he was grateful to have found a home again in this city which had embraced so many with its characteristic generosity.

He'd chosen to come to Harbin in China because there were many of his acquaintances who had already made this place their home. He wasn't disappointed with his decision; once he got here, he experienced the thriving Jewish culture that was a part of this city and felt right at home in time. Though he tried to keep his young family rooted in their original culture, he was still glad that his son Elias, an only child, was adapting to life in China well. Elias was but a few weeks old when they had come to Harbin which meant that he had little true connection with his parents' past life in Russia. Truth be told, the past seemed to recede, like a half-remembered dream, with every passing day for Mikhail too. To properly become a part of this country, he and his wife Maria were learning Mandarin; he was almost fluent in it while Maria was still learning.

The best at this language in their family, though, was Elias - this was despite, or probably because, he was so young. The thought of Elias brought a smile to Mikhail's face for his son was the one that he loved best in the whole world. He was a child music prodigy, Mikhail proudly told everyone he met these days.

At his young age, the child was already showing promising signs of exceptional talent at playing the violin, as Mikhail had unexpectedly discovered for himself a few weeks ago. Mikhail had discovered Elias's talent for violin playing by accident. He owned an old violin case – one which was very dear to him for it had so many memories attached to it from his early life – that he never left lying around at the house for fear that it might get damaged. That day, he'd taken the violin case from its resting place at the top of his cupboard to play it for a while. He was not a professional at playing the violin nor did he possess an extraordinary talent for it. Still, he had a love of music, especially of the violin; this made him want to play the instrument as best as he could – which, admittedly, wasn't very good but he didn't mind that. Taking down the violin case that day – it was rather small in size – he'd traced his hands over its rough wooden case lovingly. Then he'd opened the case and took out the violin but just then, his wife had called him over. He'd left the violin outside its case to go listen to what she had to say.

It was the sound of soft music playing that called him back from his conversation with his wife. Following the music, he came back to his room and saw that his young son, Elias, was clumsily holding the bow which was pretty large for his size. He saw as Elias put the bow to the strings of the violin and he didn't know to this day how Elias did it, but the music that the violin produced at Elias's touch sounded like magic to his ears. It was as if the instrument bowed down to this young child and yielded the secrets of its sweet music to him as it had never to Mikhail in all the years that he had tried his hands at the instrument. Instantly, Mikhail knew that his boy was born with a talent that few possess. He knew then that he needed to nurture Elias's talent till it shone; to do so was what he owed not only to his son but the world.

On seeing his son's inborn talent, Mikhail felt lucky to be living in Harbin for if there was a place that would hone his son's skill and polish him up like a diamond, it was Harbin. Known as the 'City of Music', this place was popular for its musical innovation. The Russian population of the city, incredibly talented in music, had founded the Harbin Symphony Orchestra which was one of the most well-recognised and lauded orchestras in the country.

Mikhail, along with Maria and Elias, had attended a concert of this symphony orchestra in the Assembly Hall located in the New Town part of the city some time ago. That evening, the orchestra had played the last part of Niccolo Paganini's First Violin Concerto No. 1 in D Major. That was an experience that Mikhail would remember for as long as he lived! Although Elias was barely old enough to understand things, Mikhail liked to think that he had absorbed the power of music that night and this was the reason why he was showing signs of being a future virtuoso at his early age. At present, though, Mikhail had not admitted him to any music school. Elias was barely two years old and right now, he wanted Elias to learn the Chinese language as much and as quickly as he could. As Mikhail saw it, this was the way that Elias could make his way up in this country.

Though the city of Harbin had accepted and embraced people of many languages and inclinations, for Elias to have better opportunities as he grew up required that he become fluent in Mandarin. There wasn't much effort that Mikhail or Marias had to put in for Elias to learn the language, however; Elias had picked up the language with enviable fluency at an astonishingly fast pace. Mikhail smiled again as he neared his home, looking forward to seeing his son's face and hearing his excited babble that he reserved for his father's ears each day.

Entering his modest-sized house, Mikhail was greeted by a smiling Maria. He smiled back at her as he took off his long overcoat and his top hat.

"Hello, dear. How was your day at the shop today?" Maria asked him, as she did every day.

"It was fine, *solnishka*[4]," Mikhail replied smilingly, referring to her by the Russian endearment he had always used for her from the time they had begun courting. Though they had left Russia some years ago, they still spoke to each other in their own language for it was hard, despite the violence and persecution they had suffered, to ever forget their home country entirely.

"Elias has been looking for you, Mikhail. He has asked me ten times in the past hour when his 'Bà'[5] would be home," Maria said with a twinkle in her eyes. Mikhail laughed at that, delighted that his son had missed him so much. Mikhail and Maria both viewed Elias's distinct preference for the Mandarin language at home – so opposite to what they did – quite amusing. They were happy that their son was taking to life here like a duck to water and secretly, both were proud to see the quickness with which Elias absorbed every new thing that came his way – language included.

Just then, Elias came running out of the room, wobbling

---

[4] Little sun.
[5] Father.

on his tiny dimpled legs. His curly black hair was long enough to cover his eyes. Bending down to his knees, Mikhail picked Elias up and swung him around a few times. The child's delighted peal of laughter rang out in the small hall of their house. Maria watched as both father and son made funny faces at each other, thankful to have a happy family.

"*Bàba, nǐ hǎo ma?*[6]" Elias asked sweetly.

"*I am well, my son. And how are you?*" Mikhail answered, pleased to see that his son was learning manners with as good a speed as he was learning Mandarin. Setting him down, Mikhail produced a sweet from the pocket of his shirt and waved it in front of Elias's eyes who grabbed at it with his tiny hands.

Mikhail didn't tease him for long – he never could refuse his son anything, even in jest – and handed over the sweet that he had bought on his way home. This, too, was their daily ritual. Elias was too young to register the significance of these tiny things but Mikhail and Maria both hoped that

---

[6] Father, how are you?

everything that Elias experienced in his young life would be able to give him roots, or an anchor, that would always make him feel that he belonged with his family and by extension, to the world. The small and big gestures of everyday life that Mikhail and Maria had cultivated here in Harbin were quite deliberate in that regard. They wanted to develop their own customs and personal rituals that would grant them a sense of roots, not in a place per se but with each other, which each felt they had lost as they had left Russia to settle in Harbin. Over the years, they had struggled a little in finding their place in Harbin though the city was very welcoming to their community.

Even so, it wasn't easy for them to leave behind everything they knew and adjust to a new world. The skies above their heads had remained the same but the land on which their feet rested had rocked like an unmoored vessel for a time before they finally found a steady place here in Harbin. Even now, Mikhail and Maria recalled the angry, resentful glances that some people had thrown their way when they first came to Harbin. Though the city had a sizeable population of Russians, it seemed as if the arrival of each new pair or a family brought about a fresh wave of resentment in the residents for reasons unknown to them. Maybe it was because they were Jews, Mikhail and Maria had thought. A lifetime of persecution had taught them to be wary of their status as Jews in a world that was seemingly all against them. They had even considered the option of hiding their religious identity when they had left Russia. Upon arriving in Harbin, though, they felt that the city, with its multicultural hue, would make no such demands on them. As it was, there were tens of synagogues in the city. There were several Jewish shops, hotels and other businesses – telling them that they need not hide from anyone.

Even so, it was hard for Mikhail to let go of the worries. When he had first opened his shop, he had spent half his time being worried about possible vandalism. Most of his fears stemmed not from the things that he saw in Harbin – on the contrary, this city had opened up a whole different world of safety and prosperity to him, the likes of which he had not known before – but from his earlier experiences in Russia. It was one thing to be Russian and another entirely to be a Russian Jew. Though things had never been well for their community in the country, things had taken a decided turn for worse in the aftermath of the Revolution of 1917.

Mikhail was not someone who had strong political views. He stood neither with nor against the Red Army; as he saw things, he had his own personal life which he wanted to remain removed from the political happenings of his time because he had little interest in them. What did communism have to do with him? Why should he participate in a revolution he felt he had little to gain from? He had decided to remain neutral and not get involved in the warfare and the needless bloodshed. However, he soon found out that wars do not allow for anyone to remain a bystander.

Either you are in it or you are dragged in it. He saw this very well when his extended family, of his uncle on his mother's side, was ruthlessly massacred in 1920 in the Galicia province. He had heard news – with grisly details of victims being dragged out of their beds in the dead of night and shot without mercy, of women being raped, and of even children not being spared – from the survivors of the horror that had visited so many. What had struck him most about the violence that had been perpetrated against his people was the senselessness of it all. Why were they attacked so ruthlessly? Why were they charged with disloyalty to their own country? Why were their homes destroyed as though they were sandcastles that mattered nothing? Why were they killed in cold blood? Why were those that had survived left to die of their injuries as if they were less than animals who deserved inhumane treatment? Was it only because they were Jews? Though Mikhail wanted there to be a different reason for everything – something that made sense, something that reason would accept – the voice in his head told him with brutal honesty that it was only and only because they were Jews.

As things had spiralled out of control and the violence got ever nearer to the town in which he lived with Maria, he felt that there was little choice for him but to leave. And so, he'd packed his belongings and left with Maria and Elias for they were the only family he had left by then. He didn't want them to suffer the same fate as so many others had – not the burnings, not the killings, and not the famine.

Where he lived, he felt there were more and more evils to contend with each day than there were means to fight or resist them. Then, for the peace of his mind and for the security of those that he loved the most in the world, he had made the decision to become an exile. Once he got to Harbin, though, he no longer felt in exile – at least, not for long. He had made a life here with his wife and his son. He intended to make this life last. He knew he was a common man who, in the face of violence, would be quite defenceless. He had his shop, he had his traditions and he had his wife and his son. Those were the things that mattered to him and those were the things that he wanted to protect above everything. Over the years, a large part of his extended family as well as immediate family had been killed or died; some of them had moved to the United States while he had made a choice to move here to Harbin where the culture, according to his acquaintances who lived here, was more like his home country.

And now he was here, with a past like a dark tunnel behind him, a present that he loved and a future, he hoped, that would be better than both. The voices of his wife and son intruded on his contemplation of the past. He heard them both talk to each other – Maria in her soft, melodious voice and Elias in his chirpy, high-pitched one. Mikhail smiled when he heard both of them converse with each other in Mandarin. To Mikhail's ears, Elias's Mandarin sounded more fluent and polished than Maria's who still mixed up words every now and then.

He watched as mother and son played a game where each counted numbers in three languages – Maria in English, Elias in Mandarin, and then Maria again in Russian. Maria had insisted that their son learn all three languages with fluency. Russian and Mandarin were no problem; they'd teach him Russian and Mandarin he was learning at a good speed himself. With English, they intended to hire an instructor or admit Elias to a school that would teach him the language since the two of them only knew rudimentary English.

"One!" said Maria.

"Yī!" answered Elias in Mandarin.

"Ah-deen," followed Maria in Russian, asking Elias to repeat after her.

Then Maria prompted, *"Two!"*.

"…èr!" answered Elias in Mandarin slowly this time.

"Dvah," said Maria patiently, repeating it again for Elias to remember.

In this way, they counted to ten. They repeated the exercise thrice so that Elias would remember the numbers in all three languages. Then Elias, mischievous as he was, started shooting questions at his mother in Mandarin. The little brat knew his mother struggled at the language which was perhaps why he spoke only in it from time to time, just to get a rise out of her. He loved exasperating his Mama, and to have her run after him all day long.

He was a lively, curious child who poked his nose into each and everything that he found interesting. This was the reason why, Mikhail thought, he had put his hands on the violin in the first place. Elias was so young that he had little idea of divisions or boundaries – in the way that all children don't. This was why he had so naturally, no unhesitatingly, accepted the culture and language that was so foreign to his parents but already so familiar to him.

"Mǔqīn!" Elias now screamed, laughing with a devilish sparkle in his eye.

"Nǐ zài zuò shénme, Mǔqīn?"[7] He asked.

"Nǐ huìbúhuì jiǎng guóyǔ?"[8] He piped in again, not

---

[7] What are you doing, Mother?
[8] Do you speak Mandarin?

giving his mother a chance to respond. His mother laughed at that, amused at his wit that had started to show at such an early age. She picked him up in her arms and threatened to give him a beating before giving him a big kiss on his chubby cheeks. Mikhail watched them from a distance, smiling at their mock argument. Since he loved his family like he loved no other thing in the world, he was determined to give them the very best of everything.

This was the reason why he worked so hard at keeping his shop, why he cared not for night or day when it came to his work. He knew that he had to do his best for his family – for his wife and his son, so they could have the life that they deserved. Though there were several things that were not in his control, Mikhail was adamant that he do his best to give his son the best start that he could in life.

As things were, Elias had little in the way of family to rely on as both Mikhail and Maria had little family left. There were his friends and neighbours in Harbin, the kids his age that he played with all day on the Jihong Bridge and in the streets of their neighbourhood; however, Mikhail knew that such friends were only temporary and that the real roots of any child came from his family. He was glad to be living in a country that had strong family values as he did for those were the beliefs that he wanted to instil in his son from a very young age. He just had all these plans for Elias even though he knew Elias was too young to even understand the meaning of the concepts that he had in mind. Yet, Mikhail couldn't stop dreaming dreams for his son's success in life. In his eyes, Elias was already on his way to becoming an accomplished musician when he had only put his hand on a violin once.

The heart of a father, he said to himself, wanted good things for his son so much so that he believed he could will them into existence. The way he saw it, he only had to work hard enough and his dreams for his son would all come true. Just then, Maria called him at the dinner table. Tonight for dinner, she had made rice and stir-fried Suan Cai stewed with pork.

Mikhail's mouth watered at the delicious smell wafting from the bowls that Maria was putting on the small circular table. He went to the table and put Elias in his seat before taking a seat himself. As he waited for Maria so they could start eating, he looked at Elias again. His son had a spoon in his hand with which he was clobbering the table, overjoyed at the loud banging noise that the action produced. He smiled at him indulgently, noting the child's happy disposition. At that moment, he decided to admit Elias to learn violin at the institute in the city next year when Elias would be three years old.

He felt that that would be the right time for him to start, even though it was young by most standards. Closing his eyes, he said a quick prayer and promised to himself to be the best father that he could for his son before he dipped his spoon in the piping hot stew.

Chapter 3
Catching Up

The musical evening was coming to a close. The guests were departing one by one and Elias would have left long ago too had it not been for Zhao Jiangsu. To say that this night was not what he had expected it to be would be an understatement. The unanticipated encounter with Zhao Jiangsu had shaken Elias to his core.

It was as though the past had surged up like a high, unstoppable wave that had swallowed him whole. He could no longer try and evade the memories of his early life as he had done for so many years for now the past was staring at him right in his eyes in the figure of this ageing man. Only now did Elias realise why ever since he had seen this old Chinese official with the slight built and wrinkled face he had been overcome by such a strong feeling of strange familiarity. As it was, Elias was a bit surprised at himself for not having recognised him sooner than he had.

"Jiangsu tài," Elias said, *"I can't believe you are standing in front of me. I thought I would never see you*

again."

The old man smiled in his distinct way, his eyes turning into half-moons, and replied, *"Elias, wǒ de háizi[9], life often surprises us most in ways we never expect. If you ask this old man, he would say that he had always known we would meet again. Fate never leaves connections like ours as chance meetings never to be repeated..."*

Elias nodded gravely at this, apparently convinced by the conviction with which Zhao Jiangsu had spoken the words. Inwardly, though, he felt amused laughter bubbling up in his throat at being referred to as a "child". It had been years since he was a child and certainly ages since he had been called one by anyone.

He didn't laugh, however, for he feared to hurt the old man's sentiments. He actually kind of felt happy to be called that by Zhou Jiangsu – it reminded him of the time when he was very young and had been called the same by him. Some things, he could see now, had not changed. The thought left him with a warm feeling which was almost physical in its

---

[9] My child.

intensity; it put him in mind of the sudden sunshine breaking through the clouds on lucky days in the perpetual wintry days of Harbin that he used to experience in his childhood. This morning Elias could not have imagined being in the same room with someone from his past – yet now, here he was. You never could tell how your day would end from the way that it began, Elias mused, shaking his head slightly. All through the day, he had battled the undeniable feeling of dread that had chased him like his own shadow.

He had thought the persistent feeling of anxiety that had dogged him had to do with the chances that this night's performance presented to him of rekindling his acquaintance with anything Chinese after so long a time. He hadn't wanted to do that – no, he had refused to do that with a vehement reluctance that always dominated his feelings about his past life in China.

All through the day, he had resolutely told himself he wouldn't be drawn back to the past, that he would put his foot down, give the performance he was appointed to give and then put his violin back in its case and head back home to forget the night like it never happened. He was determined to shut the crack in the door of his past life that had appeared out of the blue before it widened and the bygone times came flooding in. Yet now, as he looked at the slender frame of Zhao Jiangsu illuminated by the dim lights of the hall, he wanted to change his mind about everything. He wanted suddenly to give in: he wanted to go over his early life and examine it like a traveller explores a land that has turned foreign because he has not visited it in ages.

He recalled the quote from L. P. Hartley's novel *The Go-Between* which he had read long ago but still remembered quite accurately: *"The past is a foreign country: they do things differently there."* Elias believed that this was the truth. He now wanted to go back to his past, now that Zhou Jiangsu was here, and reacquaint himself with it in the manner of old childhood friends meeting each other in their twilight years.

Zhou Jiangsu's voice brought him out of the reverie he didn't realise he had fallen into. The old man, who had apparently not noticed that Elias's mind had wandered, continued the sentence he must have started when Elias hadn't been listening, *"....so I will say goodbye to you now. My health doesn't allow me to stay up so late at night. Old age is catching up with me, I'm afraid."* He smiled a little self-deprecatingly to show he was poking fun at his own weaknesses.

Elias looked at him again and hesitated before asking, *"Would you like us to meet somewhere in private? To catch up, for old times' sake…"* His voice trailed off and lacked its usual note of confidence as he wasn't too sure that the old man would be up to it.

He got his answer even before Zhou Jiangsu said it in words for the familiar endearing smile appeared on his face, lighting it up like a Christmas tree. He said, *"I was hoping you would say that. I didn't want to ask on my own for that might have made you feel obliged to see me even if you didn't want to. In fact, I wouldn't have faulted you for it if you had made the decision to not rekindle our acquaintance…"* Now, Zhou Jiangsu's voice trailed off. Elias looked at him then, and raised his brows in question, wordlessly asking him to explain what he had just said.

Zhou Jiangsu took this as an encouragement to continue and finished what he had started saying, *"I know it is not easy for anyone to go back down such lanes of memory that are marked at every turn by pain and loss."* He awaited Elias's response but Elias had grown utterly still and silent.

Worried that he might have scratched old wounds when he felt he had no place to do so, he looked at Elias with concern and regretted clouding his sad eyes. It took Elias a minute to shake himself out of the daze Zhou Jiangsu's words had put him into. His mind was suddenly catapulted back to the times he had always wanted to but could never forget. The luxurious interior of the music hall with its carpeted floors, majestic chandeliers and polished glass ornaments receded and then faded entirely. Before Elias's eyes, a scene appeared, marked by images of horror upon horror: the bloodied streets, the torn and broken bodies, the scorching small fires, the deafening sounds of various devices of destruction, and the pervasive smell of death.

Though he knew it to be an illusion, a mere trick of his brain, he felt he was again in the same place he had so narrowly escaped, where so many others had lost their lives. A few words had the power to conjure up the past for him so vividly that he found it hard to shake off the feeling of being pulled back in time. He could no more resist the involuntary human act of recall than a stone could resist being dragged to the ground by the power of gravity. Truth be told, Elias hadn't expected him to be so very direct about it but now when he thought about it he wasn't surprised because the old man had always been like that – he had always said things as they were and not how the other person might want them to be. Elias, for his part, felt no anger or bitterness toward Zhou Jiangsu for bringing up the past in the manner of dredging up old bones from an ancient grave. If anything, he felt this was the best way to tackle the history that they shared which would loom over them even if they tried with all their might to avoid it. Putting a smile on his face, he looked at Zhou Jiangsu and said with honesty, *"I do want to see you, Jiangsu tài. If I don't then I would regret it for the rest of my life."*

Elias saw as the words brought first a smile on the old man's face and then tears to his eyes. Moved by the sincerity of his smile and tears, Elias felt happy to have made the decision to see the man who had saved his life. He could never forget all that Zhou Jiangsu had done for him. For that reason, he could never stop being grateful to this man because if not for him, Elias wouldn't be here and he wouldn't be who he was today.

"I am going to remain in the United States for some time as I have official work. And now, I have a good excuse to stay here. I am staying at The Mayflower Hotel so we can

either meet there or make plans to see each other elsewhere if that is what you want," Zhou Jiangsu told Elias.

At this, Elias remembered he had his business card somewhere in his pockets. He always carried those cards around out of habit instilled in him at the start of his career as a professional violinist and saw no reason to break the habit even though now he needed no card to introduce him to and get him in contact with anybody.

He patted the pockets of his jacket and slipped his hand in the inner one, fishing out his business card. His name – Elias M. Abrams – was embossed in gold, boldfaced letters that set off nicely against the creamy white colour of the card. He handed the card to Zhou Jiangsu and said, *"Here, Jiangsu tài, please take my card. I want you to have this so you can ring me up anytime you want to."*

Zhou Jiangsu took the card and then examined it with the intense interest of a child who has just got his hands on an unusual toy. He ran his fingers over the smooth texture of the card and then traced the letters that made up Elias's name in the English language. Elias belatedly realised that being Chinese and having no knowledge of English, the old man wouldn't be able to read what was printed on the card. Yet he saw Zhou Jiangsu pocket the card with a mixture of enthusiasm and pride as he said to Elias, *"My boy, you have this business card as all important people do! I cannot tell you how proud I am of all your accomplishments though I can stake a little claim in them. You always were so incredibly talented at the music that I am not surprised you have got to the heights that you have – and in the United States of America, of all places! I can say that I am pleased and proud but not that I am surprised...."*

Looking at Elias again, Zhou Jiangsu paused to shake his head, perhaps in amazement. Then he continued, *"...I am not surprised in the least because I always knew you had what only perhaps one in ten thousand people are born with: a natural talent for this art of music that not even your worst experiences in life could take away from you."*

Elias smiled at that and answered, *"To the contrary, I think my worst experiences honed my skill at music. The way I see it, I came out of those experiences better at music than I was before I'd been through them."*

"How do you mean?" said Zhou Jiangsu with a perplexed frown on his face. He was all ears and obviously wanted Elias to elaborate on what Elias had just said.

Elias shrugged his shoulders in the characteristic American way that was as much a part of his personality now as his music. Then he continued, *"Who knows? If I had not gone through what I have in life, I might never have dedicated my whole life to this art. I may have become distracted by the all those things – games and girls – that young boys become enamoured of, sometimes at the huge cost of their innate talent which in my opinion they owe to the world to work on and demonstrate. For me, though, my life experiences never allowed me to stray from my violin…"*

Zhou Jiangsu nodded as Elias concluded, *"So my violin – my music – has been the one and only constant thing in my life – a life that has been shaken like a stone tossed upon rough ocean waters. So all through the years, I have clutched on to a violin with the desperation of a drowning man. After you, if I owe my life to anything, it is the violin. It saved me, Jiangsu tài."*

Zhou Jiangsu understood every word that Elias had said. He knew how most people who have suffered through unimaginable pain in life usually end up taking either one of the two paths available to them: they either go under or they rise higher. The people who fall into the second category are the ones who can use the devastation they have witnessed to create life; for him, this meant using destruction creatively. Music as an art form, Zhou Jiangsu thought, was life and life-giving. Elias had taken the second path and had emerged a winner against the demons that must plague him – the demons of his past. He was all the more proud of Elias for that. When Zhou Jiangsu had first met Elias, he was still a child; even then, his talent at music was apparent. He was glad to see that none of it had gone to waste.

"Elias, I must say that you inspire me with your love of music. To me the greatest show of resilience isn't to have never been broken – rather, it is to have been shattered into pieces but then putting yourself back together with the courage to live on. That is true grit, and not many people I know – not even soldiers, I tell you – are capable of doing that. You have done this, too, so I hope you are proud of yourself. You have not just survived your life's circumstance, you have made life bend to your indomitable will. Tài bàng le![10]*"* Zhou Jiangsu finished and slapped Elias on his back.

---

[10] Great job.

Elias could only smile in response. If that is what Zhou Jiangsu wanted to believe about Elias then who was he to stop him? In truth, life was never as easy as words can make it out to be. By the words that Zhou Jiangsu had just said to Elias, anyone would have thought Elias a saint with superhuman strength that had enabled him to rise so splendidly above circumstances. However, Elias knew his weaknesses; he knew his vices. As Elias saw it, his rise was accompanied by his fall – though this may sound like a paradox.

If Elias had a life philosophy it was that life was a not a chord progression of highs and lows that succeeded one another – no, that would be too simple a way for a thing as complicated as life made a choice, life was a polyphony of highs and lows – each high and each low was an individual melody but the two always harmonised with each other to give life its tuneful, mournful music. He didn't want to explain all of this to the old man who was almost glowing with pride at what he saw as Elias's triumph over life. He didn't want to deprive him of his rosy take on Elias's journey so he restricted his response to a smile that revealed little of what he thought of his own life and instead of communicating all his complicated thoughts, he said, *"We should meet for dinner in the next few days. I will take you to the best restaurant here in DC and then we can also sightsee around the city. You are a guest here and I want you to leave America with only fond memories to show for your time here."*

"Of course, my son. It will my pleasure to have dinner with you. We will have some time to ourselves after all these years and then you can tell me about your life here. I am most eager to learn the story of your life," said Zhou Jiangsu with a happy twinkle in his eyes. Elias laughed, and beckoned the last of the waiters who were now clearing up the hall. Taking two wine glasses from him, he offered one to Zhou Jiangsu.

Both of them raised their glasses in each other's direction and Zhou Jiangsu said, *"Gān bēi!"* Elias had heard this toast before when he was young. It strangely meant *"dry cup"* and Elias had never been able to understand why this phrase was used to give a toast with cups that were full to the brim with wine. A vague memory floated up from the conduits of his memory. The vision of his memory showed him the vague silhouette of his father – forever young in his mind – stand up from his seat on the table where he and mother and some of their friends who had been invited over for dinner were sitting. His father banged the table with his left palm loudly while his right palm was curled around a glass swirling with dark liquid; he'd then cheerily said "*Gān bēi!*" as the rest of the party shouted their approval and chugged down their drinks. Elias had watched this hidden behind the doorway to the dining room for it was past his bedtime and he was not allowed to join in with the elders.

Coming back to the present, he took a large swallow of the drink. At the same time, he quietly marvelled at the unpredictability of his memory which, at its whim, dusted off the cobwebs of some incident long ago and offered it up to him perfectly preserved.

So many of these events were ones he didn't even know he remembered, not until some remark or musical note or gesture brought it back to life for him. Zhou Jiangsu sipped at his drink carefully, not swallowing it in one go. Elias remembered he never used to be this careful with his food and drink – he'd always been one to consume deliberately and assuredly. But this wasn't the case now; Elias attributed this change to old age.

"Then we shall meet. I will call you at the hotel and we will finalise our dinner plan. I will reserve a table for the two of us at Rive Gauche – that is the best restaurant I know here in the capital!" Elias said to Zhou Jiangsu excitedly. It was for the first time in a very long time that Elias had felt so excited about anything.

"Oh Elias, I forgot to tell you. My daughter Fei – you remember Fei, don't you? – has accompanied me to the United States. She was so concerned about my health that she refused to let me wander continents away all alone. So she tagged along with me. I want her to meet you as well. We often talk about you to each other," said Zhou Jiangsu with a smile.

Elias nodded with a smile. Courteously, he answered, *"Well of course then! I will meet Fei on the same day as we have dinner. You know what I will do? I will get us a table for four. You bring Fei and I will bring my girlfriend. We will all have a splendid time together,"* he finished with a big grin. For as long as Elias had lived in America and for all the acquaintances he had made, there had never been any visitors to the country whom he could call family. Zhou Jiangsu's and his daughter were the closest things to a family for him, he thought, and he wanted to be the best host that he could be to them. Zhou Jiangsu nodded in assent and then the both of them sipped at their remaining drink in quiet companionship. For two people who had not met each other for ages, they already seemed to have a strong rapport. Both of them wanted to see where they might take their newly rediscovered connection and the dinner they had planned seemed to be the first move in the right direction to them.

Soon, Zhou Jiangsu bid him a good night. After an exchange of handshake with Elias, Zhou Jiangsu was accompanied by other delegates to the car waiting to take him to his hotel outside the music hall. Elias watched him leave and after that, he left for the limousine he had kept waiting long enough.

As he took long, sure strides towards the curb, he felt tears running down his face. He put his hands up to wipe them off. The evening was one of the revelations. His sudden chance encounters with someone he thought he had lost long ago had given him an emotional shock though he was only now feeling its effects. Despite the tears, he felt the most lighthearted he had for years. Getting into the back seat of the car, he put his hands on his violin case which was resting beside him: it was his one true and faithful companion, he thought. Replaying tonight's turn of events in his mind, he closed his eyes and quietly drifted off to a dreamless sleep.

Chapter 4
Invasion

Maria watched her son as he sat at the dining table, completely engrossed in writing on a page in his childish scrawl. He was finishing the work he was assigned at school before his father got home. Though Elias was only three years old, he took all his schoolwork seriously and was already very responsible. Hiding her apprehension, Maria glanced at the clock for perhaps the hundredth time in the last half hour.

She was awaiting her husband's return from his shop and he was late. Elias had not noticed that his father had not come home at his usual time or he wouldn't be sitting so quiet and still. Every evening, he sat at the table and completed his work before his Bàba arrived home because after that, all his time was spent with his father. If times were normal, Maria wouldn't be so anxious about Mikhail being late but in these times, she couldn't help but be worried. Just then, there was a knock at the door and Maria, breathing a sigh of relief, rushed to open it. Outside, the evening had fallen already and the sky was turning dark.

Though the days were mild in this month of September, at night the temperature always dropped. Even now, as Mikhail stepped inside, a gust of cold wind blew in their direction. Mikhail took off his coat and handed it to Maria. Next, he gave her his walking stick and hat. His eyes met Maria's but he didn't give any explanation and walked inside. Maria followed him and instead of posing any questions as to what had held him up, she asked him if he needed a hot drink to regain some warmth.

She would ask all questions later when Elias was asleep. Their child was extremely perceptive; he picked up on details and nuances that most children his age would never notice. This was the reason why the two of them always tried to reserve difficult discussions for when Elias was asleep or safely out of earshot. Maria brought a glass of hot water to the table where Mikhail was now sitting with Elias, helping him write the Mandarin letters which were pretty complicated for a three-year-old. Elias, though, was really proficient at the language and this was yet another thing that he was known at the school for. Maria sat at the table and looked on as father and son did what they did together routinely.

The sight gave her a sense of comfort and she thought, *"At least something is still normal for us."*

She watched as Elias grabbed at the pencil his father had taken from him and Mikhail dodged him playfully. The two started laughing as they played their silly game and Maria finally smiled at the happy sight before her eyes. After some time, they had dinner, which had become a meagre affair in the last couple of months. The winters this time around were bitter cold and the family was in the habit of going to bed soon after dinner. After putting Elias to bed, Mikhail and Maria retreated to their room.

"Mikhail, what is going on?" Maria said as soon as she entered the room.

Mikhail exhaled deeply before he said, *"Things are not getting any better, Maria."*

"I know that but what has happened this time? You didn't seem all right when you came in and you were late, too."

"I got talking to some of the other shopkeepers who had gathered at the corner of the street. One of them had fresh news which he shared with all of us," Mikhail said as an expression of trepidation came into his eyes.

Maria looked at his face which suddenly seemed to be covered with a web of agony. She looked away, not wanting to know but at the same time ready to learn everything in all its details. There were a few moments of quiet which weighed heavier than any words they could have spoken to each other. Maria sat on the bed and pulled up her legs. Then she closed her eyes and took a deep breath, as though preparing herself for the worst news. Mikhail, who was sitting in a chair on the side of the bed, looked at her worriedly.

"Maria, what is it? Do you not feel well?"

Opening her eyes, Maria said, *"I am fine, Mikhail. It's just that I don't want to hear any bad news. It seems as if all we get these days is bad news. How are we supposed to live like this?"*

"We will survive, Maria. But if we are to do that, we need to look at reality right in the eyes and without any fear. We are more resilient than we think, remember," Mikhail answered in a soothing voice meant to comfort Maria and buckle her up.

Resisting the urge to argue, Maria decided to confront the ugly truth head-on. She said, *"So tell me then. How are our Japanese fellows and how does their relationship with us fare?"*

"There has been an accident. Someone – Japanese or Chinese – placed dynamite on the South Manchuria Railway last night. The news that has reached tells us that no harm was done. Even so, the Japanese have threatened retaliation."

"What retaliation? Do they have any proof that it was the Chinese rebels who did such a thing?"

"I don't know what retaliation but I smell violence in the air already. And no, there is no such proof to verify the Japanese accusation but who's to change their minds? I feel as if they will stop at nothing to appease the war fever that has overtaken them," Mikhail answered in detail this time.

The mention of war had Maria sitting up straight in bed. With alarm in her eyes, she turned her entire body in her husband's direction and asked, *"Why do you say that, Mikhail? Why do you predict war?"*

"I don't predict it, Maria, but there is just something that I can feel in my bones. It's the same as last time – what we experienced back home. I can't name the feeling but it is there, nagging at my brain. It's hard for me to ignore it."

"I hope and pray you aren't right this time, Mikhail. I cannot bear to go through another war and this time, with our son with us. I will just close my eyes and pretend everything is fine and that war didn't follow us from home to Harbin. Let me be ignorant for as long as we safely can."

Mikhail didn't say anything to her after that. For months, something had seemed to be brewing in the political realm of their adopted city. Every day, news came in from different neighbouring regions, reporting small but undeniable signs of trouble which might lead to possible conflict.

Nothing had happened yet but there was a general feeling of unease that lingered in the atmosphere. People couldn't help but feel tensed over the conditions that were gradually shifting to towards instability. As Maria drifted to sleep, Mikhail remained on his chair and watched the dark sky through the small window of his room, silently praying for all his instincts to be wrong this time. The next morning, however, his worst suspicions became true.

News spread like wildfire through the city that the Japanese had invaded Manchuria. Closing his shop as soon as he got to know, Mikhail rushed home. For probably the first time, Maria and Mikhail did not take into account Elias's presence as they discussed the imminent occupation of the city. As it was, they couldn't shield their son from what would happen next. They had been through something like this and they could foretell how things would proceed from then on.

In the days that followed, they heard reports of the Japanese army taking hold of the region that was located to the south of their city. The news that came told them how the Japanese were making Manchuria their stronghold. One by one, they took over the regions that came in their path. They had taken over Qiqihar and were rapidly advancing towards Harbin.

From the way things were progressing, they knew that the Japanese army would soon occupy their city. They learned that the Japanese had made Manchuria a puppet state of Manchukuo. As they were not Chinese but Russians, they couldn't really predict what Japanese occupation would mean for them but they had little hopes from it to be of any benefit. The fear and uncertainty in the city grew with each passing day but there was nothing that they could do at present. So everyone just watched, waiting to see which way the tide would turn. Things continued as normally as they could under the circumstances – shopkeepers kept their shops, children went to school, and women socialised like they did usually – but no one knew when the fragile semblance of normality would shatter for them just as it had for other people in the region.

More and more people became resigned to the fact that the Japanese would occupy their city any day now. So they watched and listened with consternation, hoping against all hopes to avoid the painful fate that accompanies the occupation of any place by a foreign power. The occupation, when it finally happened, occurred at the beginning of the New Year.

It was January of 1932 and the temperature was bitingly cold. It was in this month that the Japanese army invaded the city of Harbin. The sounds of gunfire woke Elias up and he began crying. It took a total of seventeen hours for the city to give up. The Chinese army that comprised mostly of civilian volunteers who were neither properly trained nor armed was unable to withstand the Japanese assault which closed in on the city from the west and south. Aircraft flew down low over the city's sky and there was constant bombing accompanied by gunshots. Later, the residents watched from the rooftops of their houses as the conquering army marched triumphantly into Harbin, which was now completely occupied. They knew they were lucky to have escaped alive and that there were tough times ahead.

Maria and Mikhail knew this would happen yet when it did, it came as a shock anyway. The Japanese occupied the city but the citizens tried to carry on as they did before – that is, as much as they could. Shops still welcomed customers, women still held dinners and children still played on the streets. No matter how hard they tried, though, a very obvious change had occurred and signs of it were everywhere.

One day, Mikhail came home unexpectedly early. Elias was at their neighbour's place at that time, playing with their son who was the same age as him. Maria opened the door of the house and saw Mikhail standing there with his face stamped with an expression of horror and shock. He stumbled inside the house and without taking off his hat and coat, he staggered inside. Maria rushed after him and this time, she didn't hesitate to ask him what was wrong immediately. She had to ask repeatedly because Mikhail seemed to have run out of words. All this time, her mind conjured up the worst possibilities and her imagination ran wild. However, she kept herself under control and waited for Mikhail to answer her.

"You wouldn't believe, Maria, the terrible things the Japanese army is doing down south!" he finally burst out with his agonised eyes burning with rage. He looked tormented and Maria was scared to see him like this.

"What has happened, Mikhail? Will you tell me or make me guess?"

"You couldn't guess if you tried. These are things that I believed even the vilest human beings were incapable of doing. Our imagination couldn't conceive of all the things that I heard are taking place, Maria. I don't have words to describe the horror," he said in a hoarse voice.

Suddenly, Mikhail started to look gaunt and stooped towards Maria, as though he had aged years in the span of a few moments. Maria only now noticed that there were many more grey hairs at his temples and wrinkles around his eyes and mouth than before. Maria knew Mikhail was always worried about the safety of his family but it was only now dawning on her how worried he really was. She looked at him expectantly, silently insisting that he continue.

"Have you heard of Unit 731?" he asked her.

"No, I haven't. You know I have been trying to avoid all information I can. Although the Japanese have occupied our city, and I will for as long as I can. Why, what is Unit 731?" Maria said in a level tone of voice.

"It's a brigade that has descended straight from hell, Maria. They don't seem human at all to me. The things that they have done, the things that they are doing... I never knew the human race was capable of such viciousness, such willful cruelty," he said passionately. His face had turned red and he was shaking slightly from the effort of holding in his rage.

"We have seen the Red Revolution, Mikhail. Is it any worse than that?" Maria asked, surprised at how calm her voice sounded and how composed her demeanour was, though internally her entire being wanted to withdraw from the world so she didn't have to listen to yet another tale of

horror upon horror.

"It is much, much worse, Maria. If I am honest, then the things I've just learned make me think that this unit can put even the Red Army to shame. When I left Russia I thought that was the end of it. I didn't know the nightmare would follow me like a shadow, no matter how far I went away to escape it," Mikhail said.

"But what has Unit 731 done?" Maria asked again.

"They have done all the horrible things it is possible to do to human beings. They have not spared women, not even children. They are using human beings as though they were dispensable pieces of trash. They are cutting people up. They are burning them up in flames as though they were straw figures and not beings of flesh and blood."

"This seems too appalling to me to be true, Mikhail. Whose mind made up such a story?" Maria seemed unwilling to believe that these weren't stories but true accounts.

Mikhail said, *"This isn't a tall tale, Maria. These things are really happening. This army unit treats people as 'logs', like they came into this world to be felled at their hands. They are using people for their medical experiments, injecting them with all sorts of chemicals and exposing them to all sorts of conditions to reach so-called scientific conclusions of their wild tests."*

"How do you mean?" Maria asked.

"In the freezing temperatures of Harbin, they force people to put their arms or legs under an icy tub of water till it freezes over, locking the limb in. Then they wait the whole night to see how long it takes for the ice to thaw from the heat of the person's blood. Or if not that, they use an axe to repeatedly clobber the frozen limb, just to discover how strong human limbs really are," Mikhail said. Maria's eyes opened wide in horror at that but Mikhail wasn't finished.

He continued, *"They take people prisoners and infect them with various diseases. Then to study the effects of the disease they cut the organs out of people while they are alive and then leave them to die. They cut off limbs or they pound them to see what it looks and feels like."*

"They also crush people so they can study the injuries caused. They deprive people of food and water to see how long they would continue to live without it. They burn

people's faces to see how it looks in the end. Is this enough or do you want to hear more of their atrocities?" Mikhail asked Maria whose face had drained of all colour.

"No, I don't want to hear more, Mikhail. I want us to get out of here. You say they don't spare children. We have to take Elias out of this city. We don't want them to use our child as fodder for their war machinery!" she said with tears streaming down her face freely.

"That is exactly what I was thinking, Maria. The people here seem too optimistic to me. Perhaps it's because a lot of them haven't yet witnessed the atrocities that human beings are capable of. Even the people who heard these reports with me seemed reluctant to part with their home and their city. I wonder how they can want to stay back after hearing what they have heard…" Mikhail said.

"You are right. They might be more hopeful than we are. But having gone through it once, I would do everything in my power to make sure our son doesn't have to suffer from a similar fate. I don't want those memories of blood and death to be seared into his brain like they are in ours," Maria said.

"Elias is three years old and the sooner we get him out of here the better it will be for him. None of us wants him to have any recollection of this horrible time. We should leave here as soon as possible," Mikhail said, *"I will make the necessary preparations. A lot of families I have heard of are moving to Shanghai and Tianjin. But my cousin works at the university in Tianjin so I think that would be a better option for us. Let's make our way there. I am sure he will provide us with a place to live until we can make arrangements of our own."*

Maria nodded; she had nothing to say anymore. The things that she had heard seemed like a nightmare to her and she wanted to close her eyes and open them again to find it all gone, as though the world Mikhail has just described did not exist. But she knew she couldn't do that.

She had to look after her son and her husband and for that, she had to be strong. She would have to stare at the world unflinchingly and see it with all its ugliness. The truth was that violence and brutality wasn't anything she hadn't seen before; however, she had wished to never see the dark side of humanity again and most certainly she didn't want her son to see those things.

She thought to herself that Mikhail was perhaps right – maybe war and death had followed them all the way from Russia to here, stealthily like a cat. They hadn't been able to detect its presence and were blissfully happy carving out a new life for their son. Their time of happiness was short-lived and now like a bubble, it had burst.

For the next few days, she watched as Mikhail prepared to leave the city where they had started to feel at home. She had made friends there and her son had made quite a name at his school even though he was so young. Mikhail had established his shop which was thriving before the Japanese invasion occurred. But it was all for nought. They had to pack up their bags again and depart this city, too. She felt as if she was a rootless being, a ghost, who would never find a place she could really call her home again without it being snatched away from her.

Mikhail made short work of selling his shop. During such times, it was inevitable that he would have to sell everything at a very low rate. As it was, during the occupation of the city, all the shopkeepers had to pay a very high amount of protection dues. Mikhail also knew how the Japanese army had set up gambling dens and opium houses and brothels in all the towns they had until now occupied. He just didn't know how to protect his family from all the horrible things that were taking place. In the end, Mikhail suffered quite a heavy loss but took what he could. The lives of his wife and son were much more important than any business though he had invested everything he had into it. When all the preparations for moving to Tianjin were made, Mikhail and Maria packed up the few belongings that they had decided to take with them.

It was important that they travel light; no one during wartime could carry everything they owned with them. Even so, Mikhail didn't forget to take his old violin with him when strictly speaking it wasn't a necessity. He knew his son Elias's talent and wanted him to have the violin with him always.

Saying goodbye to the city was harder than they had imagined. They said their farewell to their friends and then to the place they had called home for the past years. This was yet another start to a new life for Mikhail and his family. It seemed to him that they couldn't settle anywhere for long, as though fate would have it no other way than to fling them from here to there. However, Mikhail was determined to shield his family from the horrors of war and for that, he had taken this risky decision of moving to the free city of Tianjin. As he left the house behind Maria who was carrying Elias in her arms, he turned to take a good last look at it.

His instinct told him he wouldn't return to this city and this house but no matter what happened, this place would always have a special place in his heart. He shut the door firmly and taking Maria's arm, began to walk down the new road of their lives.

Chapter 5
An Old Friend

Elias woke up after a night of fitful sleep. All through the night, he had had endless dreams of shadows that metamorphosed into more shadows. Though Elias tried to recall what he had dreamed of, he could remember no images but only the elusive, persistent feeling of dread that had chased him all night.

Shaking off the fog of listlessness that enveloped him, he got off the bed, throwing the covers to the floor in the process. He walked to the window lining the wall to the east. He was barefoot and felt the coldness of the marble floor which woke him up a little more. Sunlight was sifting in through the white curtains which he yanked apart to see that the day had fully dawned.

He had a bad hangover from last night; he didn't even know how many drinks he'd had before calling it a night. His head felt heavy, as though he were Atlas shouldering the weight of the skies not on his shoulders but on his head. His mouth felt as dry as cotton and he couldn't bear the sunlight that felt like pinpricks to his eyes. He closed the curtains and went to the kitchen. Twisting the tap open, he put a glass underneath the gushing water. In succession, he downed three glasses of water. He had quite a day ahead, he knew. Today, he was going to meet with Jiangsu tài and he knew he had to be in good condition to make a good impression on the old man. Thankfully, they were going to meet for dinner so he had time to recover. He had no appointment during the day so he knew he could sleep away the rest of his lethargy, if he needed to, before dinner time.

Collapsing on the recliner in the lounge, he put his feet up on the table. It was rare for him to have nowhere to go today and had all the time to himself. So right now, he didn't know how to while away the time. He picked up the newspaper that was a day old and flipped through the pages. The news was the same as always – of political discords, cultural collaborations, accidents and catastrophes, sports and the entertainment world. Life was so banal, he thought, as he skimmed over the notable events of the recent days. He felt utterly disinterested in the things that he read, as though he existed independent of the world and had nothing at all to do with its happenings.

Just then, the phone rang. The sharp trill of the phone call that had come at an unexpected time surprised him so much that he dropped the papers to the floor. He stared at the phone for a few seconds as though it were a foreign object then reached over to pick up the receiver. It was a good thing that the telephone was on the small side table next to the recliner, he said to himself. As soon as he put the receiver to his ear, however, he wanted to slam it right back down.

The husky voice of his longtime girlfriend Lois came travelling over the waves, annoying him to no end. He was surprised that he had ever found her voice to be one of the most appealing things about her; lately, he only felt irritated by it. The unanticipated and unwanted call spoiled his already bad mood.

"Ah, Lois. What a time to call," he said dryly in response to her cheery greeting.

"Why, did I wake you up?" Lois said, not letting Elias's surly temper get in the way of her enthusiasm. For the life of him, Elias couldn't understand how she could be so chirpy at this time of the day when his brain was barely able to function.

"Kind of," he answered, not entirely true. Then he cut right to the chase and said, *"What's up? Why did you call?"*

"What do you mean? Can't I ring you up whenever I want? I thought we were long past the time when I had to worry about what time I called you…" she said coyly. Her voice trailed off, hinting to him that she was waiting for him to concur with her.

He ignored her and said, *"Sure, whatever you want to think. So, what is it?"*

Lois was not deterred by his unreceptive behaviour. She was as stubborn as they came and wouldn't let a little hostility sidetrack her. *"I called you to ask about last night's performance, darling. How did it go?"*

Elias suddenly remembered he'd promised Jiangsu tài he'd bring Lois to the dinner. This meant he had to be nice to her just now, if he didn't want her to throw any tantrums, which she would if she sensed he needed her to be there at the dinner. He knew she would hold it over his head if she suspected Elias needed her. He knew he had to pretend he was inviting her only as an afterthought if he wanted to avoid the drama that Lois loved as much as she loved herself.

Modifying his tone so that it was friendlier, he said, *"Yeah, the performance. It went well, really well. I wasn't expecting it to, to be honest,"* he said. Then, adding a note of cajolery in his voice, he said, *"You know how it is when I'm not in the mood to perform."*

Lois saw Elias was being approachable all of a sudden and attributing the change to his frequent mood swings, she happily answered, *"What nonsense, darling! Even when you're not in the mood you're the best violinist out there. I wish you wouldn't undermine your own talent like this."*

Not bothering to explain that he was doing no such thing, Elias said, *"I met the Chinese official in whose honour the evening was arranged. Do you know what I discovered?"* His voice had turned into a whisper as though he were exchanging a secret with Lois.

"What?" Lois answered in an eager tone.

"The man is someone I know from before, from the time that I spent in China," he said.

"Oh," said Lois, unable to hide the undertone of disappointment from her voice. She had expected to hear some high-level gossip and not some personal tidbit of

Elias's life which he never shared with her anyway. *"I know so little about your former life, darling, that I don't know which man you speak of. Is he an important person?"* she asked.

"To me?" questioned Elias.

"No no, I mean important in the political arena," she clarified then bit her tongue at giving herself away.

Lois's answer was nothing less than Elias expected of her. He knew she only continued to stay with him, despite being as bored of him as he was of her, merely because Elias was well-connected. Lois was a bit of a social climber and she knew letting Elias go would be a poor decision for her social station in life.

This had become apparent to Elias a long while ago but he'd still not broken it off with her – perhaps because he was accustomed to her presence and felt it would take too much of an effort and cause needless drama if he ended his relationship with her. So he had decided to continue until it was absolutely necessary for him to remove her from his life.

"Yes, he is important, of course. Why else would they send him to lead the delegation?" he knew just the right

things to say to Lois.

"Oh, right. So, did you talk about old times?" she said, clearly wanting to sound interested.

"Not really, but I am to take him out to dinner tonight for official reasons," he lied.

"Wonderful. Where are you going?" she said.

"To Rive Gauche," he answered.

"Then you're taking him to the best place in the Capital," she replied.

"I sure am. His daughter is also going to join us. She's accompanied him to the States," he explained.

"Wouldn't she be bored in an all-male company?" Lois said, hinting that he should invite her as well. She had taken the bait just as Elias had wanted her to.

"You know, you are right about that. Would you want to join us? Or wait, let me ask my secretary first…" Elias answered.

"I would love to," she cut him off, *"Why bother your secretary, darling, when you have a girlfriend?"* She laughed gratingly.

Elias forced out a laugh then telling her the time – along with strict instructions to be ready at the said time without entertaining any notions of being 'fashionably late' as she was wont to do – he hung up the phone, breathing a sigh of relief. The short call had left him feeling drained and he already felt anxious about spending the entire evening in her presence. Hoping the presence of Jiangsu tài and Fei would balance out the evening, he got up from the recliner to make himself some breakfast.

***

The evening descended on the skies of Washington. Elias had called up Zhao Jiangsu to confirm with him the timings of the dinner. He also told him that he'd send his driver to pick him and Fei up and drop them off at the restaurant. He intended to take the cab himself and had told Lois to make her way to Rive Gauche on her own which she didn't mind doing at all.

Tying the knot of his pinstriped tie which matched the colour of his coat, Elias looked at himself in the mirror. Fine lines had started to appear at the corners of his eyes and mouth and his hairline was receding a little. He was still strikingly handsome, however, to invite the attention of women of all ages. The signs of approaching middle age only made him look more mature and sophisticated. He had inherited his looks from his father but his eyes were his mother's – so every time he looked at himself in the mirror he was reminded of her. He put the cufflinks on the cuffs of his dress shirt in place then pulled on the dark blue blazer. Then he combed his rather long hair and sprayed his usual cologne till its spicy scent diffused in the air.

His preparation for dinner was complete. Putting his wallet in the inner pocket of his blazer he exited his apartment, looking forward to the dinner. He was, surprisingly, quite excited to meet Jiangsu tài again as well as being reintroduced to Fei. It was surprising because he had not expected himself to be so optimistic about anything or anyone to do with his past – and yet, he was.

He hailed a cab, got into it and directed the driver to take him to Rive Gauche. There was the usual amount of traffic on the road and soon, he was at the restaurant's entrance where he had already reserved a table for four. It wasn't easy to get a reservation in so short a time but Elias was one of the regulars at the restaurant and the owner thought well enough of him to make space for his party of four in his famous restaurant which was a favourite of the top brass of the country, including the Kennedys. The host welcomed him very professionally and politely and led him to his table. Walking through the dimly lit hall, he saw many famous and familiar faces and nodded to them in greeting. He had been sitting at the corner table, which was rather secluded from the rest of the dining area, for about five minutes before Lois arrived. He got up to greet her and was bestowed with two air kisses before Lois took a seat.

Resisting the urge to turn away from the cloyingly sweet smell of her perfume, he endeavoured to make small talk with her until his guests arrived. Thankfully, he didn't have to talk a lot as Lois was busy scanning the hall and commenting on each guest that was of any interest to her. He pretended to listen to her but all the time he was distracted, glancing at his watch.

Soon, he saw the host leading Jiangsu tài to his table. A slim and tall woman accompanied him. It was obviously Fei. As she neared and Elias got a closer look at her, he could see she looked much like she had in her childhood – she was just as pretty with large eyes and a small nose that made her look younger than her years. Her long dark hair was parted in the middle and curtained her face, giving her a youthful look. Both Zhao Jiangsu and Fei were dressed in grey Mao suits, which was the formal wear in their country. As they passed, many heads turned to look at them though foreigners were in no way a novelty at Rive Gauche. Elias warmly greeted both Zhao Jiangsu and Fei. He was genuinely pleased to be their host tonight. Even Lois's presence couldn't dampen his spirit.

After the guests were all seated, he asked them if they'd had any problems so far in America. Since he was speaking in Mandarin, Lois looked at the three of them in a bewildered manner, as though she were the foreigner rather than Elias's two guests. Elias translated what he had said to them for her; though he had only invited her out of convenience, he didn't want her to feel out of place or unwanted.

To his surprise, Fei answered in impeccable English, though she had an Eastern accent: *"It has been good so far, Elias. Your countrymen are great hosts."*

Elias smiled at her and thanked her. He enquired of Fei about her life in China, what she did and her interests. This wasn't just small talk for him – he rarely indulged in that – but he really wanted to know all about Fei. For some reason, he was interested in her life; perhaps it had to do with his childhood association with her. As he talked to Fei about the current relations between China and America, he discovered she was well-informed about the policies of the American government. She was also quite well-versed in the cultural history of his country which he found rather extraordinary since he had assumed the Chinese were too isolated and inward-looking to be so knowledgeable about other countries.

As he talked with Fei, he could notice Lois staring at him from the corner of his eyes. He knew why. She was most certainly surprised by his enthusiastic conversation with Fei. Elias was a reticent man and he was, even after years, still taciturn and aloof with Lois. Seeing him so engaged with Fei must have given her quite a shock, Elias thought.

Soon, it was time to order dinner. Elias helped his guests select from the menu. This restaurant served haute cuisine and, he assumed, it was his guests' first experience of French food so he said,

"The food here is prepared by the best chefs in town, Jiangsu tài. Here, let me help you order the best that they have."

The starters were all delicious, whetting their appetite for the main course. For himself, Elias ordered Challans duck, foie gras poached in Rivesaltes, and crispy pear. For Jiangsu tài, he suggested Chicken Basquaise because he remembered his love for spices. Fei ordered Steak Diane while Lois went for her usual Coq au vin. They ate quietly for the most part; the silence was broken by Elias asking Jiangsu tài every now and then if he was enjoying his meal.

The dessert, too, was had amidst light conversation. The two women talked to each other but Elias could see that Fei and Lois were as different as night and day. They didn't really have any common grounds and could only make conversation that was a little awkward and stilted. He was still happy that Lois was trying to make his guest feel at ease and intended to thank her for it later when the evening was over.

Zhao Jiangsu's sharp eyes noticed that Elias had had more than enough alcoholic drinks tonight. He thought that was uncharacteristic at a formal dinner but didn't say that out loud. Fei and Lois didn't seem to detect that Elias's complexion was beginning to get ruddy which was a sign that he was becoming intoxicated. Zhao Jiangsu did give him credit for holding his drink well, however, as Elias barely let it show in his mannerisms that he was quite drunk by the time the dessert was cleared away by the waiter. After that, the two men ordered coffee while the women declined it. Lois took Fei to "powder her nose" and finally, for the first time tonight, Zhao Jiangsu was alone with Elias.

Elias had lit a cigarette and had offered one to Zhao Jiangsu as well which he had turned down. Now watching Elias smoke, he was reminded yet again of the child he had been when he had last seen him in China. Zhao Jiangsu had seen enough of the world at his age to know that there was more to Elias than met the eye. Last night, he had been swept away by emotions and had seen little else beyond what he wanted to see but tonight, he had realised something was up.

Tonight, he has spent all the time observing Elias. He had seen him be an attentive host, who had done everything that he could to make his guests feel welcome. He had also perceived the intangible tension between Elias and his girlfriend Lois who, he privately confessed, he did not like one bit. And he had seen Elias turn the conversation resolutely away from his past life in China though, many times both Fei and Lois had asked a question that related to his time there. To those queries, he had given only generic answers that concealed rather than revealed his life with his parents, Zhao Jiangsu felt. As the evening progressed, he realised that all was not well with Elias as he had so blissfully assumed. There was something dark and heavy that lurked behind the smile in Elias's eyes. There were ghosts of the past, Zhao Jiangsu felt, which still haunted him. When the women left, he took the opportunity to question Elias. And as was his nature, he was very direct about it.

"Elias, wǒ de háizi[11], what's wrong?"

Elias was taken aback at this question. He smiled and answered, *"What can be wrong, Jiangsu tài? I thought the dinner was splendid!"*

"The dinner was good, I don't refer to the evening. I refer to your life. You seem sad, desperately sad to me..."

Elias was, once again, taken aback. He was at a loss for words and so remained quiet.

Zhao Jiangsu continued, *"I hope you won't try to deny it, Elias. This old man's eyes cannot be deceived. I know you*

---

[11] My child.

are unhappy. Is it because of the woman in your life?"

Elias had to laugh at that. Lest the old man take it as an insult, he was quick to assert, *"Lois has nothing to do with it, Jiangsu tài. I don't let her affect my mood at all."*

"Ah, it is not Lois but something else," Zhao Jiangsu said. Elias saw that he had walked right into the trap. Now he didn't see how he could talk his way out of it without offending the man who had saved his life and who, as per the Chinese tradition, still considered himself responsible for Elias's life. And as Elias saw it, he owed Jiangsu tài a life-debt.

"What would you like me to tell you, Jiangsu tài?" Elias said with a resigned smile on his face.

"What is wrong, Elias, my child? I can see you are trying to drown your sorrows in alcohol," Zhao Jiangsu said concernedly.

His paternal worry reminded Elias of his father, whom he had lost too soon in his life. He was touched to see Zhao Jiangsu so concerned. The truth was that ever since he had got to America, there had been no one who had worried for him like a parent.

He'd had to take care of himself on his own and had become used to being answerable only to himself. That this old man, who had seen him after ages, cared about him so much brought tears to Elias's eyes.

He answered, *"I will tell you, Jiangsu tài, but I am scared to lose your good opinion of me."*

The old man shook his head strongly and said, *"Nothing you tell me would ever make that happen, my son. Just tell me what's wrong. I will try to understand."*

Elias couldn't help but confide in the old man.

He said, *"You said I 'drown my sorrows' in drink and you aren't wrong. I look only for oblivion, Jiangsu tài. And for that, I go to drinks. I go to drugs. I'd take anything that would make me forget. You see, the past was too painful for me to live with at the start. So I started to indulge in drugs and drinks. And now, I am in too deep to get out of it…"*

Zhao Jiangsu was heartbroken to see Elias's state. He was alarmed but didn't let it show. He knew he would have to talk to Elias in private somewhere and counsel him. He could see Elias was lonely. He knew he had to do all that was in his power to rescue Elias from himself.

He patted Elias's arm and said reassuringly, *"These things happen, son. Don't let it get to you so much."*

Just then, he saw Fei and Lois making their way to the table. So he quietly said to Elias, *"We will talk about this later, son. When we are on our own, away from possible intrusion."*

Elias nodded. He knew he could not resist the old man's plea to help. If he was honest with himself, he was overwhelmed by the feeling of gratitude. He had wanted help for a very long time. He had been too proud to ask for it and no one else had ever been invested enough in his life to know that he needed help. Jiangsu tài, on the other hand, had taken all of two meetings to know the state of his heart. Did old connections run this deep, Elias wondered.

Not finding an answer to it, he pasted a smile on his face and waited for the two women to take their seat. He knew he would soon have to confront his weaknesses for he now had someone who wanted to look out for him. He said to himself, 'It has been a long time coming' and then gulped down his remaining coffee.

Chapter 6
Marco Polo

"May I come in, Mother?" Elias's voice came floating on air. Maria turned to look at her son whose face was red with cold as well as his excitement for the upcoming mischief he was no doubt looking to carry out. Elias was now a little over six years old and, as Mikhail had always boasted, quite bright and quick for his age.

The door of their house located in the north-western part of Tientsin was open, letting in the noise of the rather densely-populated neighbourhood that they lived in. Elias had come home from his school through the winding, twisting streets of the inner city. The year is 1936.

They had been living in Tientsin for a little over three years now and in this time, their family has learned to adjust to the rhythms of this new city which wasn't a lot different from Harbin – no doubt because of the sizeable Jewish community they had found there. Though their living conditions here weren't as comfortable as they used to be back in Harbin – owing to their abrupt departure from that city – they'd learned to make do. After leaving Harbin, Mikhail had moved into his cousin's house in Tientsin with his family. Though his university teacher cousin was a gracious host, neither Maria nor Mikhail had felt comfortable being his guests for too long; they didn't want to thank him for his help by becoming a burden to him. So Mikhail had worked tirelessly to use what meagre funds he had to reopen his shop – albeit a much smaller one than he had in Harbin. He had the acumen for business and there were supportive people in his community whose encouragement helped him get back on his feet.

In a matter of a few months, they had been able to move into their own place and this is where they had lived for the past several years. Maria and Mikhail made the decision to get Elias admitted to the only American school in the city called the Tientsin American School. Studying there, they believed, would prepare Elias to become a cosmopolitan citizen of the world instead of a stateless refugee, a status that the both of them had been relegated to ever since they had escaped Russia. They had regrets about how their lives had turned out despite their best efforts. So they really wanted to secure Elias's future by doing whatever they could to set him up for a good life. They had hopes that this school which was run by the American embassy would secure Elias's induction in the educated strata of the Chinese society. So now, Elias spoke English fluently along with Russian and Mandarin. Even now, he had addressed his mother in crisp English that came out of his mouth as though it were his mother tongue – but then, Elias spoke Mandarin as it was his mother tongue as well which only indicated to his proud parents how gifted he was at learning languages.

"Come inside, Elias. Don't keep hanging like a monkey on the door in this weather or you'll just catch a cold!" Maria scolded Elias as she grabbed his arm gently and led him inside the house. Elias giggled excitedly. Maria could tell he was bubbling with excitement – he clearly had something to tell her.

"There, now," she said, pulling him down on the sofa to sit beside her. *"What is it that you want to tell me?"*

Elias's eyes widened in surprise. He looked at Maria and in an amazed tone, asked, *"How did you know I had something to tell you?"*

"By magic! I can read your mind, Elias," Maria teased,

laughing at the expressions on Elias's face. Looking suspiciously at his mother, Elias said, *"I do have something to tell you, Mama! My music teacher Mr. White gave me the 'extraordinary' grade today! He told me I am the best student he has taught in years and years and years!"* His voice became high-pitched and breathless during his narration of what his teacher had said to him, as it always did when he was really thrilled about anything.

Maria beamed at the teacher's words of praise for Elias. Of course, she and Mikhail both knew Elias's exceptional musical talent but it was gratifying to know that experts and teachers were beginning to really appreciate Elias's brilliance.

In Tientsin, their lives, Maria felt, had become somewhat more confined than it had been in Harbin. This was because each country's expatriates or refugees had their own little 'concessions' in the city – these were small pockets where different nationalities lived life their own way, mostly isolated from locals as well as other foreigners. Back in Harbin, they had mingled much more easily with whomever they wanted. This was why Elias had been able to learn Mandarin so quickly, because he had grown up playing with

Chinese children who lived nearby. In Tientsin, however, there seemed to be invisible lines that separated them from people who were unlike them. Mikhail and Maria had little problems with assimilating in the country's culture – in fact, they had wanted to put down roots and be a part of this country by welding their own customs with the Chinese traditions – but that hope had dwindled as they moved to Tientsin where people tried their utmost to preserve their old life and old ways of living.

Maria thought about all this as she sat with Elias for an early dinner and then helped him complete his homework before putting him off to bed. She had a lot of time on her hands here as Mikhail worked long hours – longer than he ever had in Harbin. It just seemed that the more they tried to get their life back in order, the more difficult it became for them to plant their feet on solid ground.

Maria thought of the Japanese occupation of Manchuria and said a quick prayer of gratefulness for having left Harbin for Tientsin before things became really bad for them there. Maria went about putting the house back in order. Elias had run around pulling down cushions and pillows and piling them on top of each other, so the end result looked like a row of sandbags. This is how Elias played soldier – by ducking behind the sandbags for cover in between brandishing his 'rifle', which really was the wooden soup ladle he'd stolen from the kitchen for his self-amusement, at imagined enemies. Mikhail didn't particularly approve of this game that Elias had come up with as he saw this not as a game but a simulated foray into the subject of violence and warfare.

However, there wasn't much they could do to deter Elias for then he'd ask questions and keep asking them till he got his own way. So the both of them had accepted this as the unavoidable consequence of growing up in a country which, in spite of their prayers to the contrary, seemed to descend closer and closer toward the vortex of war with each passing month.

Maria picked up the newspaper which was a few days old. It was called the *'Nash Golos'* which was Russian for "Our Voice". Maria especially enjoyed 'The Jewish Page' of this daily and would often read it to while away the time. The cultural news section reported about the events to be held at Gordon Hall, part of the British concession, as well as at the Club Kunst, which was the Jewish social club where Jewish population of the city convened to mingle.

It was a place where men played cards and billiards and women played mahjong and perused the collection of books in the reading room. Maria often went with Mikhail to the club. In such times of conflict, being with people who were like yourself, with similar worries and sorrows and joys, made her feel like she wasn't quite so alone in the world.

***

Elias's seventh birthday was the happiest one of his life. On that day, his father and mother took him out to dinner and then to a musical concert that had been arranged in the city at the most opportune time. He remembered how his father had dressed in a dark brown suit that had become a little shabby and a fedora hat that was crumpled at the edges. His mother had put on a beautiful pink dress that made her look paler and prettier than usual.

The musical concert was attended by several musicians, who his parents seemed to know and love. Amongst all the renowned and unknown artists, there was one whose face Elias would remember years later. More than his face, he'd remember the soulful music he played.

The song that this young musician called Hwang Yau-Tai played was wordless. It had no title. *'It looks to be a work in progress,'* Elias heard his father whisper. Even so, the tune was heaven to Elias' ears. The sweet, hopeful melody stirred him, and made his heart leap like a bright flame. At that age, he could not understand the bittersweet feeling that the song evoked in him – but he would years later.

During the performance, Elias watched as his father reached toward his mother's hand and entwined his calloused fingers with her pale, delicate ones. He saw the two of them exchange deep, smiling glances. They looked so happy, so beautiful at that moment. This image of his parents remained in his memory forever, with the beautiful tune of Hwang Yau-Tai playing in the background.

After the concert ended, Elias remembered walking hand in hand with them, his father on his right and his mother on his left, past the yellow waters of Hai-ho Canal. The weather that night was warmer and they were out on a family walk, just enjoying a quiet time together.

"What are you going to be when you grow up, Elias?" his father had asked him.

"A soldier!" Elias had shouted.

He remembered his parents exchanging a glance with each other. Even then, he had been aware of his parents' strong aversion to everything related to the war, even though the two of them had never said it in so many words to him. He recalled that he had laughed then, startling his parents who really had believed what he had said. He was pleased to have succeeded in tricking them this one time.

"Violinist! I am going to be a violinist, Bàba!"

His parents had visibly relaxed. They had started to smile and then laugh – in relief or in happiness, he didn't know.

"That's my boy!" his father had said as he'd picked Elias up in his arms. Though he had grown a lot by now and was tall for his age, Mikhail had picked him up as though he weighed no more than a baby and kissed both his cheeks. Elias had turned his face away – after all, he was seven years old now and wasn't a child anymore! But his father had only laughed harder at this and had kissed him a few more times to annoy him more before finally depositing him on his feet again.

At the moment, that sparkled like diamonds in the darkness of his memories, Elias had learned how much his parents had wanted him to become a musician. He had learned what he could do to make them happy. And if there was one thing that he had ever wanted to do in his life it was to bring a smile to his parents' face, to make his mother and father laugh out loud, and to see them happy as though they had all the treasures of the world resting at their feet. This was his parents' dream for him and he had, at that young age, determined to make it come true.

***

One early Thursday morning of July 1937, when Mikhail had yet to leave for the shop, their neighbours told them the rumour – for the news was yet to be confirmed – that the Japanese and Chinese forces had clashed near the city of Beiping. They knew that the areas to the north, east and west of Beiping were already under Japanese control. Yet they had hoped for the two opposing powers to maintain a truce around the city. They had also pinned their hopes on the presence of the 29th Route Army, a part of the Chinese army, which had garrisoned in Beiping and Tientsin, to prevent any outbreak of violence in or near their city.

It seemed that it was not to be, however. Later during the day they found out that it was at the Marco Polo Bridge, which they called the Lugou Bridge, where the two armies had come head to head with each other. This bridge was constructed over the Yongding River which lay 15 kilometres southwest of Beiping. Mikhail had told Maria months ago that the bridge held a lot of strategic importance for both the armies. It seemed that this fight over it was unavoidable. They only hoped that it won't escalate too much and would end in a truce, reluctant though it may be.

From all the information that they had received till now, however, it seemed to them that the Chinese army refused to back away in the face of Japanese belligerence this time. This was the day that the tentative, fragile peace that had been maintained for years finally shattered. The war between China and Japan had begun in earnest. This was the day that Mikhail had feared for a very long time. And now that it had arrived draped in the colours of inevitability, he felt resigned to it. Was there anything at all that he could do to make the river of time take a different course? To him, everything that had been happening in China seemed fated – as though the course of events had been determined long, long ago, before he was even born. And now, like chess pieces that have little will of their own, he and his family were to be manoeuvred across the board mercilessly. This, too, was something that he already knew. Within days, the situation had deteriorated beyond their worst imagination. There was no official report but news travelled fast of a major offensive being launched by the Japanese forces against Beiping and Tientsin. Mikhail heard all the news with a sense of horror descending upon him. The day that he had always dreaded, for which he had left his settled life in Harbin, had now caught up to him. He knew with certainty that he and his family will now be dragged into this war which wasn't theirs. He knew not what they would lose but he knew the cost would be higher than he was willing to pay.

They heard tales of intense fighting. They heard that the Chinese military had planted landmines to stop the advance of the Japanese troops. However, the Japanese forced past those too. They heard news of school students being handed rifles with hundreds of rounds, and of young boys being armed with sabres and grenades. Untrained, these adolescent boys were recruited to fight off the experienced and lethal Japanese forces who knew and showed little mercy to their opponents. They heard there was hand to hand combat. They learned that for every one Japanese soldier killed, there were ten or more Chinese boys left dead or badly wounded. As the weeks progressed, they learned of the massacre near Dahongmen where a cavalcade of Chinese soldiers was ambushed by the Japanese army who made quick work of killing them off. They heard how the Lieutenant General of the division was found dead in the backseat of his bullet-ridden car, having received fatal wounds to his chest and forehead.

There were several such stories of carnage and brutality that they heard during those long, long weeks when news came – sometimes travelling fast as forest fire and sometimes trickling down like desert rain. There were long stretches of time that they received no information and were left entirely in the dark as to what was going on near their own city. They didn't know how much the Japanese army had advanced and if they would invade and capture their city as well. Barely twenty days after the Marco-Polo skirmish had started off, Beiping fell to the Japanese. They heard that the triumphant Japanese forces, drunk on their victory and the blood of countless dead, marched into the city and forced the defeated nation to celebrate their victory with them. They were asked to dance and party and deliver the banzai cheer as though their own people had not become fodder for the war machinery to facilitate this success for the occupying powers. It was at dawn the next day that the city of Tientsin fell to the Japanese. It began with the assault of the Japanese marines who attacked the port of Tanggu. A simultaneous attack was launched on the city.

The Chinese units of the 38th Division fought valiantly and many local people also volunteered to repel the attack. Mikhail and Maria were confined to their home and could hear no sounds of the fighting that was taking place just on the outskirts of the city. Yet they knew the violence that was being perpetrated. The very air smelled of death and a pall hung in the skies as though to herald the beginning of the end for so many of the citizens of the city of Tientsin.

They learned that the Chinese army was able to recapture the Station from the Japanese forces that had taken hold of it. They heard that they 38th Division put up a big counteroffensive to the belligerent Japanese forces that seemed unwilling to give up. There were attacks from the Chinese forces at the headquarters which the Japanese had set up at Haiguangsi and the Dongjuzi airport. The airfield that the Japanese had set up was attacked and several aeroplanes were destroyed. In the end, though, it was not enough. Nothing, it turned out, was enough to stop the Japanese offensive. The real terror which Elias would remember began after Japanese reinforcements arrived. This was when the tide turned firmly in favour of the Japanese. All through the day and night, the young Elias covered his ears to block out the sounds of shelling and bombing.

His ears were trained to hear and appreciate music – he wanted still to immerse himself into the harmonies that he so loved but peace was nowhere to be found. There was just the stuttering of the guns that made his heart pound and then leap into his throat like a frightened little puppy. He fell asleep to the angry rattle of guns and woke up to the deafening sounds of explosion.

The aerial bombing of the city had begun in earnest. There would be no going back now. Mikhail sat stone-faced in the kitchen, waiting for their fate to find them where they were. He knew that at present, he could not gather his family and run away to a safe place. He knew the city was surrounded by the Japanese who would cut down to pieces anyone they saw escaping. He also knew that as they were living in one of the concession areas of the city, they would be granted some reprieve by the Japanese army who would treat them like foreigners and wouldn't mete out the same punishment to them as it would to the locals. Thinking of possible punishment made Mikhail shudder. It made his blood run cold as though it were slowly freezing over with icy dread. There was a sense of finality that he felt, as though the gavel had come down to pronounce death upon everyone. He had to shake this feeling off himself, however. He knew he would do anything much – in the manner of grasping at straws like a drowning man – to keep his family safe from all danger.

The city of Tientsin fell in the early morning hours. Later, they learned of the dead bodies of Chinese soldiers that had been left to rot in the scorching heat of the sun just outside the city. They learned of the broken bodies, the bloodied faces and the torn limbs of the young men who had given up their lives for their country. The artillery and air support that the Japanese received bolstered them up for the final lap. The city was captured on July 30 and once again, Mikhail found himself running into the same destiny that he was running away from all his life. Mikhail knew that he could no longer protect Elias from witnessing the horrors of war. He knew his son would see blood flowing in the streets like water. He knew he would see limp and lifeless bodies littering the streets as though they were no more than scarecrows that had mysteriously found their way out of farms and were now scattered across the cities of China. He knew Elias would see the hard facts of life though he had wanted always to protect his son from ugliness and darkness that the human race was capable of and so mercilessly perpetrated on one another.

The smoke from the burning buildings still hung in the air when Mikhail went out two days later with Elias in tow. Mikhail couldn't help but wonder if mixed in with the smoke of burning buildings was the smell of charred bodies put to fire. He wouldn't put anything beyond the invading army. Maria was at home. She was preparing to depart this city, as Mikhail and she had planned to do as soon as it was confirmed that the Japanese would soon occupy it. Their life, yet again, was unravelled. And yes, Mikhail had once again decided to pick up whatever he could and go somewhere he could rebuild it. He would do that over and over and over again if need be and if that was what it took to give his family a safe home away from marauders and occupiers who shed innocent blood like it was nothing. He had decided to go to Nanjing, for that appeared to be a safer place than here to him at this point in time. In a few days, he would take Maria and Elias and abandon this sinking ship of a city. Elias would always remember that day he went out with his father. This was the day that he witnessed firsthand the destruction of the fallen city.

This was the first time that he saw violence as close to himself as though it were his own shadow. He remembered feeling disoriented as he saw the buildings that were intact a few days ago now lying in a pile of debris. Smoke rose in the distance, darkening the horizon even though it was daytime. The thick black clouds made him think of a volcano erupting. He knew, however, that it was no volcano. He was, for the first time, becoming familiar with destruction.

He didn't know that soon, he would be in the midst of death. He didn't know yet that he would watch the black smoke rise up and pervade his whole world, and that he would have to do so without his father by his side to hold his hand and make everything all right again.

Chapter 7
Demons

"Now it's squeaky clean, just like it would be if I put it in the dishwasher a good three times!" the cleaning lady who visited Elias's apartment thrice every week said, beaming at the result of all her hard work. She had just cleared up the mess that Elias created in the days she hadn't come to put the house back in order.

Elias laughed and said, *"It sure is, Mrs. Norton. Thanks for saving the day. You did me a great favour right there, taking time out for me on such short notice,"* The middle-aged lady smiled back, pleased to have received a compliment for putting in all the work.

"The one bad quality that Mr. Elias has is that he moves through his house like a tornado. He just always leaves a wreck which I have to clean up after him. Other than that he's a wonderful employer. Really, Sally, I couldn't ask for better. He pays handsomely, and is handsome and charming, to boot! When he wants to be, I mean," Mrs. Norton had said to her friend just a week ago.

And all of it was true, for the most part. There was obviously more than one reason why she happily worked for this temperamental artist. As long as she had worked for him, she'd never had him give her any trouble like so many of her other employers did.

"He's a bit of a fry, though. Isn't he, Norma?" Sally had said to Mrs. Norton in response.

"Oh no, Sally. He's just a bit of a drinker. Doesn't seem to be able to help it. He does drink like a fish at times but I've never seen him out of control," Mrs. Norton had confided in her friend who worked at another apartment in the same building.

She'd come today to clean up Elias's house though this wasn't one of her days because Mr. Abrams had requested her to. He'd even sent a car to pick her up! She couldn't say no when he'd asked so nicely. He was apparently entertaining some foreign guests and these were sudden plans that he'd made on the spur of the moment. He needed her to put his apartment in place so he could invite his friends over. Assured and secure of her needfulness in this place yet again, she picked up her purse from the sideboard in the lounge and walked over to the door.

"All right, Mr. Abrams," she said while picking up her purse. *"I'll catch you on the flipside. I guess you'll need me to come in tomorrow or the day after to clean up?"*

"Yes, Mrs. Norton. I'll give you a ring," Elias said politely, following her to the door and then opening it and holding it for her. Beaming again at his gentlemanly conduct, she stepped out and waved him bye. Elias closed the door behind him and turned around to take a critical look at his home. He wanted to see how it would look to his guests. He'd invited over Jiangsu tài and Fei to his place for lunch this afternoon. He'd asked them last night as they were leaving Rive Gauche. Unfortunately, Lois had heard him and had invited herself over as well. Frowning at her impending unwanted presence, he surveyed the house with a searching eye and approved of what he saw.

His apartment was pretty much a bachelor's abode with no feminine touches to lighten up the sombre interior. The colour scheme was predominantly dark brown with furniture of the same colour used everywhere; there was some off-white thrown in here and there, perhaps to reduce the overall impression of heaviness. The furnishings were sparse and the open area looked wider because it was so devoid of clutter. It seemed like an impersonal space, as though no one lived here permanently. There were no photographs on the wall, no special artefacts, and no odds and ends strewn about that marked the place at his own. Elias had not created this effect deliberately; rather, it had happened unconsciously. Years of moving around like a nomad in his childhood had instilled in him the feeling of never being at home anywhere. So even though he'd lived in America and in this particular apartment for a number of years, he'd experienced a lasting feeling of homelessness. So he'd lived here like a wayfarer, someone who never got attached to a place for who knew when he'd have to pack up his bags and leave for good.

The more he looked at the interior of his apartment with the eye of someone who'd be visiting it for the first time, the stronger became his view that his house looked more like the inside of a bar than a home. Of course, the bar installed at one end of the living room strengthened that impression. For a few minutes, he considered the idea of going for a renovation sometime in the future then dismissed it. He didn't particularly care about how his house looked. As for his guests, he hoped neither of them would have the same or similar idea that he'd just had about his apartment and even if they did, he hoped they wouldn't share it with him. Assured that the place was presentable, he called up the catering service that he'd booked to deliver food. Having reminded them, he had little else to do than getting ready for lunch. When Jiangsu tài and Fei arrived, he welcomed them with a smile and genuine happiness. Lois was going to be fashionably late, as was her wont, and he was happy to have a few moments alone with his guests. Asking about Jiangsu tài's health and whether or not Fei liked it here in the city of Washington, they had a good time before the doorbell rang, souring Elias's mood a little though he had expected the arrival of his so-called girlfriend.

Like a good host, he pasted a smile on his face – this was not to flatter Lois but to show his guests from China that he hadn't lost his manners here in America – and opened the door to find Lois dressed to the nines for what was, after all, only a casual lunch. Perhaps she wanted to impress the guests, Elias thought with a snigger which he was careful to hide. He watched as she approached Jiangsu tài and bent down to hug him, as though he were an old friend of hers. Caught by surprise, Jiangsu tài kept his hands to the side as Lois wrapped her arms around his small figure.

His eyes widened and Elias turned around to hide the fact that he was openly laughing. Then, Lois walked to Fei and hugged her as well. Fei took it a lot better than her father and smiled back at Lois though a bit impersonally. Elias smiled at that and only liked her more for her polite but indifferent demeanour toward Lois.

"Darlings, I'm so excited to see you again today. We had such a good time last night, didn't we? Well, of course we did!" Lois answered her own question excitedly. She had a habit of doing that, carrying a conversation all by herself. Even now, the two people she was supposedly conversing with only nodded and smiled back politely as she really didn't seem in the mood to give them a chance to speak.

"Elias here has never introduced me to any of his old friends, did you know that?" she said, wriggling her brows as though she was sharing a juicy bit of detail with them. *"You two seem like a novelty to me. As a bit of a rare treat, you know. And you two do look so exotically foreign! That's just icing on the cake,"* Lois said with a high-pitched laugh. Her manner was completely breezy; apparently, she thought nothing of the words she'd said. A look of displeasure crossed over Fei's face at Lois's speech. She was offended

by the implicit condescension in Lois's tone and obviously didn't like being compared to a rare and exotic 'treat'. Elias could sense as she frosted over and became more formal than she already was with Lois. He understood the reason why. And why wouldn't he? He'd been through the same when he'd first come to America. Though he didn't sport the same Asian features as his guests, which made it easier to label and then proceed to treat them as strange beings, he was still every bit of a foreigner when he'd first arrived in the States.

People had noticed that and had made him feel even more of an outsider with their behaviour till he finally got better at camouflaging himself in the crowd. He'd found that offensive and since then, he had developed a serious abhorrence for the kind of exoticisation toward people from other cultures such as the kind Lois was displaying at present.

He rushed to change the topic lest Lois's ignorance spoils his guest's time at home. As he tried initiating a conversation about arts and music in America and China and how the two countries could collaborate on a cultural scale to improve the relations between their citizens, he noticed Jiangsu tài glancing at him, his eyes full of questions. Elias could already tell what his questions would be. The caterers rang the doorbell then and Elias was saved by food. After they'd had their lunch, Elias realised that today was one the day of the meeting, the day he had long put off, the day he would have to accept he was powerless over alcohol. He had signed up a few weeks ago but hadn't yet gathered enough courage to visit. Now that Jiangsu tài was here, he felt like he could go. He wanted the old man to see that the words of comfort and encouragement that he'd said to Elias ever since they'd met were starting to give positive results.

Not thinking too much about it, he decided to leave Fei here with Lois – he trusted her to hold her own with Lois and give as good as she got, if the need arose – and take Jiangsu tài with him to the group meeting. He got the car keys and told the three of them he had to show Jiangsu tài a famous place. They didn't protest and Jiangsu tài got all excited about the trip, too. Wondering where he thought Elias might take him – there really was nowhere for them to go but down memory lane – he walked to Fei to reassure her he'd bring back her father intact. She told them to have a good time and smiled brightly. Reading the very contradictory cry for help in her eyes, he swallowed the laughter that bubbled in his throat and left the apartment with Jiangsu tài in tow. They got in the car and Elias started to drive. Once they got on the road, he turned to the old man and asked, *"Do you have any questions for me, Jiangsu tài? I can see that you want to ask me things. Please don't hesitate."*

Zhao Jiangsu remained silent for a few moments then said in a very straightforward way, *"I am a little worried about your choice of a woman, Elias."* He talked in the typical manner of Chinese elders who wouldn't think it was interference or prying to ask about your romantic interest in life. Elias appreciated the honesty as Zhao Jiangsu quickly added, *"Not that there is anything wrong with Lois. She seems like a good girl but just…"*

As his voice trailed off, Elias said, *"Yes, Jiangsu tài?"*

He said, *"She is nothing like you. She isn't sensitive the way you are, wǒ de háizi. Why didn't you find a woman who was more like you?"*

Elias heaved a deep sigh and answered, *"I don't really know, Jiangsu tài. Let me think about it. You know it's been so very long since I first started dating Lois. Even I don't remember the reason why I began seeing her back then."*

After a few moments of thought Elias said, *"I think I began dating her because I was lonely and because she pretended to care. I met her at a bar, you know."*

"Then?" asked Zhao Jiangsu, clearly interested to know all about it.

It was a rather novel and unnerving feeling for him to have a listener. Perhaps because of losing his family and never having someone close enough after that, he had grown up to be a rather quiet and private person. He was in the habit of keeping his joys and sorrows as well as his troubles and anxieties to himself. But now, he had a listener – someone he trusted and who cared about him enough to want to know all about him.

So Elias began to unearth the feelings he'd long ago suppressed and began talking. He was surprised to discover it wasn't as difficult for him as he'd thought it would be. It seemed that Jiangsu tài had a way of putting Elias so completely at ease that he let down his guard and confided in him things that he'd never even really admitted to himself.

He continued telling him the story of how he'd met Lois. *"I had gone to New York for a leg of concerts. I used to be with the Radiance Symphony Orchestra back then. I remember how during those concerts I used to perform the Gold and Silver Waltz by Franz Lehár. Those are some fond memories I have, I liked being with those people,"* he reminisced.

"Anyhow, it was one of those particularly tiring days. I needed a break so I went down to the bar of the hotel we were staying at. I got myself a martini and as I was sipping on it, I heard a woman laugh. I just liked the sound of it. It perhaps reminded me of someone though I still don't know who. It was just the sound of her voice which got me interested in her. I turned to my right and saw a stylish woman sitting two seats away from me. She was joking with the bartender, laughing at one of her own jokes. Lois has always been like that," he laughed. *"She noticed me looking at her. She gave me her signature thousand-watt smile and I became instantly infatuated with her."*

"Oh, so it was merely an attraction. How long have you been with her?"

"For around three years, I think. The infatuation, of course, died long ago. I know it's too long a time to stay with someone you don't love and don't even like, now that I think about it," Elias said with honesty. It was for the first time that he'd admitted not liking Lois to anyone out loud.

"So why are you still with her?" Zhao Jiangsu asked quizzically. As far as he was concerned, these things were pretty clear-cut. You liked someone, you stayed with them. You didn't like them, you broke it off and moved on. That's how you found someone you really loved so you could marry them and have a family together.

"Out of habit, I suppose. I have been very lazy about my relationships. I don't really invest myself in them, or try harder at making them work. Of course, having a partner like Lois who is so different from me doesn't help. I think she'll be happier with someone else but for some reason, she's still in this relationship. We clearly don't know where we are going with it," Elias said with a short laugh. It felt good to come clean about all the things that had bothered him for some time now.

"Why?" the old man asked.

"Why what?" said Elias.

"Why do you not invest yourself in relationships?" he asked.

Elias was taken aback. He didn't realise when he'd said what he had said. And now, he was thinking about his own words, turning them over in his mind time and time again, like you run your tongue over a sore tooth unconsciously. He peeked at Jiangsu tài and saw him looking at him expectantly. *"I guess…I don't invest myself because I am not sure they'll last…"* his voice trailed off.

"Why wouldn't they?" Zhao Jiangsu asked piercingly.

"When have they?" he asked in return.

"You mean you fear people leaving. Isn't that it?" the old man said, displaying razor-sharp insight into the workings of Elias's mind.

Elias was struck by surprise once more. He remained silent, not knowing what to say. He had staunchly been avoidant when it came to analysing the reasons for his behaviour in his personal relationships. He'd known something was wrong but he'd never tried on his own to get to the root of it himself because then that would have to be followed up with practical steps to fix the problem. Seeing him silent, Zhao Jiangsu said, *"I think it's because you were wrenched away from everyone and everything you knew and held dear in your early life that you developed this fear of people abandoning you. It happens, I can understand. I think the issue was worsened because you never found someone who'd shared similar experiences and who you could relate to."* This seemed to be a perfect and neat summary of the emotional block that Elias had suffered from ever since he'd come to America. It was, in fact, messier than this but this was the gist of it.

"Yes I had a pretty rough time of it, I can admit that," Elias said at last.

"So you turned to vices…" the old man said. There was no judgement in his tone or in his eyes, only compassion and understanding. He, from personal experience, knew what it was like to always live with a burden upon your soul, with a grief so heavy that it weighed you down like gravity.

"I turned to drink," Elias inclined his head in simple agreement. He didn't deny it for he didn't want to lie to the old man who had nothing but empathy for him.

"Does it help?" Zhao Jiangsu asked.

"It did, at first. Every time I felt the old memories rushing back, I would drown myself in it. It brought me forgetfulness and I was tired of being so wide awake all the time. I just wanted to dim those memories, Jiangsu tài. All the screaming, the blood, the pain. I had to subdue it so I could live," Elias said with devastating candour.

"My child, I am so sorry," the old man said with sorrow written on his face.

"Thank you, Jiangsu tài. You know, it was difficult for me to survive in this world of music in the beginning. It was really hard, I can admit that now. I had no one who had my back. There was no one who'd sponsor my education in music. Other artists I know went to Paris and Brussels and Vienna to study music. I never could do that. I didn't have the resources back then. I had no father. Looking at others, I missed my father so much. I remember how he always did his best for me all his life. Even though I had nothing but natural talent in music, I decided to do my best to make it," Elias said.

"And you did," the old man said with a proud smile.

"I did. There were a lot of things that I had to sacrifice. Sleep, peace of mind, leisure. But I knew I had to fulfil my parents' dreams. You see, I couldn't let them down," Elias said.

"And do you not think that too much reliance on alcohol can cost you all that you have achieved? I have seen many a man first drown his sorrows in his drink and then drown himself in it," Zhao Jiangsu said with worry clouding his eyes.

"I am trying to get better. I have to tell you this, I got the final push because of you. I have wanted to give it up for a long time. I wanted to stop drinking. It became like a demon that possessed me, that got hold of me and didn't let go until I gave in to its whims. I didn't like losing control of myself. Even so, I could just not take the final step. I am doing it now. We are going to a meeting where people who have a problem with their alcohol assemble. I am going there for the first time, I hope you don't mind coming with me, let's see how it goes," Elias explained.

Zhao Jiangsu nodded his head, approving of the visit to the group. There were a few moments of silence in the car when each man sat lost in his own thoughts. Elias stared out the window screen but his mind was elsewhere. He was thinking about how the second half of his life had started – all the things that had happened to bring him to where he was today. In his mind, there was a clear divide – there was a 'before' and there was an 'after'. The 'before' time of his life included all the years that he'd spent with his parents, brief though they were. The 'after' time included all the years up to now that had come after their deaths. As he thought of his parents dying, he felt an excruciating pain that blinded him for a moment. He stepped on the brakes suddenly and the car stopped.

"What happened, Elias?" the old man asked worriedly. He had his hand on Elias's shoulder and was looking at his with concern.

Elias caught his breath and said, *"I just had a flashback about my parents' death. I haven't thought about it for a long time. I buried it all because it was difficult for me to cope with it. They came back just now and…it still hurts me as much as it did the day that I lost them both."* Elias had tears in his eyes and so did Zhao Jiangsu. The old man patted his back and in a minute or two, Elias regained his composure and started driving again.

"It might help if you talk about it, Elias," Zhao Jiangsu said as they got back on the road.

"I do want to tell you, Jiangsu tài. It's been too long for me to have kept it all bottled up. And if there is someone in the world who can understand and who will appreciate my parents' sacrifice for me, it is you," Elias said with gratitude in his eyes. He was undoubtedly thinking of all the past times when Zhao Jiangsu had helped him without asking for anything in return.

"Yes, my child. So how did it happen, Elias? How did your parents die?" Zhao Jiangsu asked.

Elias took a deep breath and then began to tell the most painful story of his life.

Chapter 8
Safety Zone

Elias woke up as sunlight streamed in through the small window which had no curtains to keep the light out. He opened his eyes and proceeded to close them tightly as if doing that could keep the world and its grimness at bay. He could already hear his mother puttering about in the kitchen – or what paraded as a kitchen in their one-room hut. Elias knew she was preparing their breakfast. Since they had got here to the capital city of Nanking, breakfast had become a meagre affair. Elias recalled the sumptuous meals his mother used to make back in Harbin and then in Tientsin, though even there they had had to skimp like they'd never done when they had lived in Harbin.

Maria approached Elias with the intent to wake him up and saw him make an annoyed face with his eyes still closed. She let out a laugh at that, amused at her son's antics. She said, *"You may get up from the bed now, Elias. There's no use trying to go back to sleep when the sun is looking straight into your eyes."*

Elias shot up on his bed as soon as Maria finished talking, as though he were a doll with springs attached to its body. *"It is staring right into my eyes, Mŭqīn! As if I stole its food!"* Elias complained exaggeratedly. Lately, Elias had become rather theatrical. He'd exaggerate his words and movements. Sometimes, he'd pantomime all through the day. For the most part, Mikhail and Maria were amused at his theatrics.

However, they were also sad because they knew this was Elias's way of coping with the abrupt change in his life. They also knew Elias was old enough to decipher the lines of worry on his parents' faces that had become a permanent now. They knew Elias had become more playful to compensate for the lack of peace and joy in their lives. So he carried on his clowning just to make his parents laugh.

"Come on, up now, solnishka. We've got no time to waste!" Maria said, willing away the anxious thoughts that had begun to creep in.

Elias got up and went outside the small hut to wash up. Mikhail was already up and had already had his breakfast. Lately, he had become quiet, very quiet. Within days of the fall of Tientsin to the Japanese army, Elias had told Maria to pack up only their most necessary belongings. He had not asked her or discussed the matter of shifting with her – he had just told her that they were moving to the capital city of Nanking for their safety.

At that time, Maria had argued with him. She'd said, *"But we can't keep running forever, Mikhail. The Japanese are everywhere. What guarantee do you have they won't in a few months or a few years come to Nanking and occupy it as well?"*

"There is a possibility that they won't. I have collected some information from people I know. They have told me that a lot of families are moving to Nanking because the city is safer. It is the capital of the country, Maria. The Chinese government will do everything they have to so that it doesn't fall," Mikhail explained.

From the determined look that shone in Mikhail's eyes, Maria knew it would be futile to argue with him. She actually wanted to believe him; she wanted to have hope that there was some corner of this country that would prove to be a safe haven for them. However, all the years of roaming about like a nomad had left her exhausted. Mikhail thought Nanking would be safe and she didn't want to oppose him only to find out he was right. So, like she'd done so many times before, she packed their belongings and left the city that she had called home for a small three years. This time, though, Elias was old enough to object. He'd even resisted the move, trying to make them see how he had his violin lessons here and that they couldn't possibly expect him to go to a new place and make new friends and start lessons all over again. For the first time in his life, Mikhail had been angry with Elias. He had not scolded him but he had been very stern as he had said, *"Do as you are told, Elias. I will not tolerate any arguments."* Thus the matter was 'resolved' and their family of three had fled to Nanking.

The city of Nanking greeted them with dust and mild weather. It was the second week of the month of August and the temperatures in the day were fairly warm. At nights, the temperature dropped and it became cool. There was no way to feel at ease in the city, Maria had thought on her first day here. Like their family, so many others had fled to Nanking. They were under the same belief that Elias had shared with Maria, of Nanking being a safer place to be. The city seemed to be brimming with people. Maria felt claustrophobic even when she was out in the open air.

Her immediate and intense dislike of the city was exacerbated by the fact that Mikhail hadn't yet found a way to set up shop here, as he had in Tientsin. At the start, they'd had to make do with what little savings they had. Living in a small, rudimentary hut which didn't even have curtains on its windows had made Maria somewhat bitter. She, however, had not lost hope. She still told herself everything would turn out to be fine. *'It will only take a few days, and then we'll be back on our feet,'* she'd often reassure herself.

She had pinned her hopes on Mikhail's determination and resourcefulness which had prevented them from financial collapse many a time. Here, too, when he could not find enough means to start his shop, he had started to work in one. It was a big step down for him but he did it every day for them, without complaint. Maria couldn't be more proud of and grateful to him.

They had not been in Nanking for a week when news came of the Battle of Shanghai. Elias and Maria had heard from their neighbours who were in dire straits just like them. This 'Pearl of the Orient', as the city of Shanghai was called, had become a bloody battlefield. They found out how the murder of a Japanese officer a few days ago had sparked what they now knew would be another campaign of carnage. They did not know the details of the fight but they knew that the results would be death and destruction. Silently, guiltily, Maria had hoped the Japanese army's war lust would be quenched by attacking this major city of China. She had prayed for the Japanese to leave Nanking alone. Trying though the circumstances here were, at least they were alive and with each other.

Time passed like it always does. The country remained in turmoil but they had become accustomed to that by now. Elias felt listless in this city; perhaps that was because here, he didn't go to school. He had little to occupy his time. Most days, he spent playing with his new friends who, like him, were idle. Sometimes, he'd take out his father's old violin and play it for them.

The first time he did that, his friends were amazed. None of the little boys and girls that he had made friends with, were musically talented, so Elias with his violin which he played like a grownup was a novelty to them. They often requested Elias to play for them but most days he refused. He was still angry at being taken out of school though he never voiced his opinions to his father. It was during the last few days of the month of November that the atmosphere of the city began to darken. It was as if a huge cloud of doom had come over the skies of Nanking, heralding the end of life in the city as they knew it. Mikhail kept up with the news from around the country but a lot of times, he tried not to share the particularly gruesome details with Maria. He didn't want to upset her; he wanted her to live in hopes of better days. He, on his own, was quickly losing hope. The city of Shanghai had fallen to the Japanese. Everyone knew that the Chinese forces had given up the city to the enemy.

Mikhail was responsible for his family and they depended on him entirely. But the way things were going down in the country, it seemed harder and harder each day to protect them from the violence that the Japanese had unleashed with full force. He feared what would happen to this capital city of Nanking. He'd come here believing this was a safe place. The Chinese would protect this city at all costs. But now, after the defeat at Shanghai, he wasn't sure about that anymore. He also knew the widespread destruction being perpetrated by the Japanese army. He knew they had razed entire villages to the ground, while blocking all means of evacuation through ship or road.

He shuddered at the thought of having all escape choked and prayed things would not come to this should the Japanese decide to head to Nanking. More and more, it seemed to him that the day would come to pass when they'd be under attack, too. Then with the arrival of December came the news they had not anticipated: the Chinese government was relocating the capital of the country. The high-ranking officials left the city on December 1, as the people watched, helpless to do anything.

They watched as the president departed the city on December 7th. Then began the bombing of the city. Mikhail's worst fears came true: there was no getting away from this city that he knew would soon become a slaughterhouse. Normal life, or its pretence, crumbled away – not slowly but all at once. There was nothing for the people to do but wait for their fate to find them.

Mikhail's hut was located in a small district in the southwest of the city. In the nights, silence descended like a blanket in their neighbourhood only to be tattered by the piercing, deafening sounds of shelling. The exploding shells greeted mornings as well. Just outside the city walls, preparations were underway for the attack which was now imminent. The citizens, those who remained, were prepared to face the worst. However, not even in their wildest imagination could they have predicted what would befall this city once the Japanese launched their attack. The inevitable happened on December 13th. The remaining Chinese troops were no match for the bellicose Japanese side. The massacre began. Mikhail and his family lay clustered in the corner of the small hut, having heard many tales of the advance of the Japanese forces and their acts with unbelieving ears.

Mikhail cursed the day he had decided to move here. He felt his panic escalate with every passing day. His family didn't know that guilt choked him like an invisible tightening noose. In his hurry to protect his family, he had unwittingly led them right to the slaughter.

Though he knew Maria would say he couldn't have known – and he knew this, too – he couldn't help but beat himself up about moving to Nanking which was now going to go up in flames. The last vestiges of hope in his heart for his family's survival kept him alive. He sorely regretted not leaving the city when they could have. A large number of people had fled while they could but he hadn't, along with many of his neighbours. This was mostly because by this time, all of them were so poor that they couldn't afford to move. It required money to make one's way out of this doomed city and Mikhail had not a yuan left to his name. So he'd remained here and this was the outcome of that decision. The city was already reigned by chaos. The bombing was now constant. There was a complete breakdown of order. Criminals abounded and looting had become a normal occurrence.

The Chinese troops had already been forced back by the unrelenting Japanese attack that came from all sides. Attacks were launched on the western side of the city where lay the southern banks of the Yangtze River, and on the southeast side as well. The carnage of the Chinese soldiers began when Japan's Central China Front Army entered the city.

Mikhail knew there was a safety zone hastily delineated in the city and he decided to take his family there. On the night Mikhail and his family were to leave the hut they lived in, two Chinese soldiers knocked on the doors of their house, asking if they could stay the night as boarders. Mikhail let them in as Elias and Maria watched from the corner of the only room. One of the two soldiers was badly injured; to Mikhail, it didn't seem that he would survive for long, at least not if he remained holed up here instead of receiving medical aid. The uniforms of both soldiers were torn and bloodied. Their state screamed the reality to Mikhail's family: there was more of the same horror to come. The soldiers – whose names were Zhao Jiangsu and Wen Jiashou – told them how some of their comrades in the Chinese Nationalist troops had tried to escape the massacre by crossing the river but the Japanese warships had opened machine gunfire on them.

They were positive that no one had survived. They also divulged that many of the Chinese soldiers had shed their uniforms and wore plainclothes now to evade the killing that would come their way if they were recognised as soldiers of the Chinese army.

"The soldiers' fate is sealed. If we remain here, we look to death that has become as certain as the fact that the sun will rise tomorrow. But there is still some hope for escape," the soldier called Wen Jiashou said to Mikhail.

"You don't look Chinese to me," the other soldier Zhao Jiangsu said as he leaned back against the wall of the hut, trying to make himself comfortable.

"We came to China from Russia many years ago. This is our home now," Mikhail explained.

"This is a very unlucky time to be Chinese, my friend," Zhao Jiangsu answered, shaking his head regretfully.

"You look foreign to us. Hopefully, you'd look similarly foreign to the Japanese army. Go to the safety zone. There is one near the American embassy, run by a foreigner just like you," Wen Jiashou, no doubt meaning to be helpful.

Mikhail felt a sharp stab of pain at being so casually called a foreigner though he had spent years in this country trying to build a life here and to give back to its people. He didn't argue his point, however, and only said, *"Yes, yes. I am taking my family to the safety zone. We depart tonight."*

Zhao Jiangsu who looked to be the older and more mature of the two said, *"Better hurry. Take the first chance you find to get out of this city. You must know all escape routes are being clogged by the Japanese one by one."*

The injured Wen Jiashou added, *"The Shuixi Gate to the south is being manned already. They say it is to prevent the soldiers and smugglers from escaping but we all know it is meant to cage the civilians, too."*

Elias heard this exchange in its entirety. He watched his father try to remain calm. Even then he knew he would never forget the horror and pain that came in his parents' eyes hearing the stories of looting and murder. He'd never forget the pain and horror in his parents' eyes as she heard stories of women being carted away, not even in the dead of night but in the middle of the day, by the Japanese soldiers.

So Elias along with his mother and father left the hut to the soldiers and made their way to the safety zone which they knew was their last hope to survive. They left at night with only the clothes on their back and Mikhail's precious violin. They had walked several miles in the dark and silent night when they suddenly saw a bright glare. This came from a fire that the Japanese no doubt had set to one of the houses in this locality.

The ferocious blaze leapt higher and higher in the air. In the orange glow that it shed on their faces, Elias saw tears run down his parents' face. He was too shocked by the sight to cry himself. He remained quiet and tightly held his mother's hand. He knew he would be safe as long as he was with them.

"Quickly, quickly, hide behind the hedge. Lay down on the ground," Mikhail whispered with panic in his voice.

Elias and Maria automatically did as he asked. The hedgerow on the roadside was big enough to hide all three of them. They crouched uncertainly, hearing the jarringly merry voices of an approaching group of Japanese soldiers. Mikhail peered above the hedge and saw as one soldier in the group rapped briskly on the door of one of the houses on the street.

The door was opened by a man. His face was illuminated for a few moments but before Mikhail could register anything more, the Japanese soldier leading the group brandished his bayonet in the air and proceeded to drive it right through the man's stomach.

Mikhail let out a gasp and watched with his eyes wide open in shock as the soldiers kicked the man's writhing body out of the way and entered the house from where he could hear a female shriek drowned by the sound of the soldiers' laughter. Mikhail turned around to look at his family and saw that both Maria and Elias had followed his lead to look over the hedge. They, like him, had witnessed the murder. Maria had her palm clapped over Elias's mouth to prevent him from screaming. She herself was gasping. She was breathless, as though she had run up and down a mountain. The senseless violence that they had just watched had left them reeling. Mikhail felt all the energy drain out of his body. His heart was beating so fast he felt it would jump right out of his chest. He put his arms around Maria and Elias, trying to make them disappear from view. His instinct told him his time with them was up.

Elias didn't know how much time passed. The only thing that registered in his mind were the agonising screams that came from inside the house – the voice of a woman desperately pleading and then crying in pain, the high-pitched cries of a baby that broke off suddenly, abruptly. *'What happened to the baby?'* Elias would later remember himself thinking.

The woman's voice died out after a good long time. Elias didn't know then but their voices would haunt his dreams for as long as he lived. For what seemed like an eternity, the soldiers remained inside the house. The rest of the street was deserted. Perhaps there were people inside the other houses but they had no way of knowing that. As the group of soldiers emerged out of the house, the firelight fell on their faces, giving it a devilish glow. They were laughing amongst themselves, as though they hadn't just now eradicated a family from existence. The prone body of the man lay on the doorstep of the house, as though guarding it even in death. One soldier kicked the body out of the way unceremoniously and the group began to make its way down the street. Mikhail or his family couldn't see the soldiers coming near as they lay huddled behind the hedge but they could hear them come near. Their rapid conversation in a language they did not understand was punctuated by raucous laughter that grated on Mikhail's already frayed nerves.

The sounds instilled terror in Elias's heart which felt frozen to him. He watched as his mother who was holding him tightly trembled uncontrollably. His father looked equally terrified. In the looming shadows, he saw his father's face: he had his teeth tightly clenched and sweat was rolling down his face. It looked as if he was willing the Japanese soldiers to go the other way, to not come near his family. This, however, did not happen. Perhaps they heard a noise or perhaps they saw their shadow, but in the next few moments, one of the soldiers was standing right before the three of them, pointing his bayonet at Mikhail.

He whistled before declaring in Chinese, *"Look who we have here!"*

Then turning to his companions, he barked out something which Elias couldn't understand.

"You!" he said to Mikhail who was trying to hide Maria and Elias behind them. *"Stop cowering like a coward and stand up!"*

Mikhail remained silent and still for a moment but then he obeyed. He felt he might be able to gain some mercy for his wife and his son if he did everything the soldiers told him to. He pushed himself to his feet and bowed.

"Hah! Look at the peasant bowing to us. That's right. We are the ones in charge now. That's exactly how you should behave," the soldier said. The rest of his entourage didn't look like they understood Chinese but they nodded their heads eagerly at every word this soldier said.

"Please, sir. We are not Chinese. We were making our way to the safety zone. We are civilians. Please let us go," Mikhail begged. Behind him, he could hear Maria start to cry softly.

"But you speak Chinese. So you are Chinese," the soldier decided.

Mikhail shook his head but the soldier pushed him aside. He was now directly looking at Maria and Elias who were shuddering in fear. Mikhail had never felt as helpless as he did in those moments. With his eyes fixed on Maria's trembling, crying form, the soldier said something to his companions. Two of them lurched toward Mikhail and abruptly seized his arms as the third launched his bayonet in the air with a flourish, as though it were a show.

The two soldiers holding Mikhail's arms pushed him down on his knees. The last thing that Mikhail saw were the faces of his wife and son. The last thing he heard was their scream which rang through the night air.

Elias watched as the soldier hacked violently at his father's head. He saw a fountain of blood splash out of his father's pierced neck and fly in all directions. He saw his father's bulging eyes and heard him scream, a sound that was completely unknown to him before that day. He saw as his father's head lolled this side and that before it was completely severed from his thrashing body.

Elias screamed and screamed and screamed. He got up on his feet and ran toward his father. Before he could reach his father's body, one of the soldiers grabbed his arm in a painful grip so that he was dangling high above the ground, kicking his heels, trying to get the evil man to let him go. He turned his face toward his mother and watched as she struggled to stand up on her feet.

He saw as she finally got up and ran toward him, screaming his name, but before she could get to him, the soldier threw Elias on the ground. Elias's head thudded painfully on the ground and began to throb. Before Elias could get back up on his feet, the soldier put his boot on Elias's stomach tightly and then bayoneted him, too. Elias felt a sharp pain run through his entire body – unbearable, excruciating pain. Then his world became dark. There would never be light again.

Chapter 9
Guilt Of The Past

Elias opened his eyes and watched the empty road through the rain-stained windscreen. Beside him, he could hear Zhao Jiangsu breathing. The old man was quiet and still as though he had been struck into motionlessness by a binding spell. As Elias had related the story of his parents' death and the days leading up to it, he had lost track of time. The car was parked on the side of an almost-deserted road and there was little traffic here. It took Elias a minute to recover from the onslaught of memories that seemed bent on drowning him forever.

He had, perhaps for the first time since coming to America, taken a trip down memory lane. The edges of his vision became dark as he, once again, thought of all that had been done to the people he loved the most in the world.

"Elias, my child," began Zhao Jiangsu.

Elias turned to look at him. The older man thought that Elias looked like he had aged centuries in the minutes that he had recounted the most terrible time of his life.

Unbeknownst to Elias, there were still pieces in the story missing. He had, Zhao Jiangsu thought, been spared the pain that came with complete knowledge. There were still some dark passages in his memory maze. He couldn't recollect everything because he didn't know everything – and Zhao Jiangsu wasn't about to enlighten him. For instance, he knew how his father had died and he knew that his mother had died but he didn't know how exactly his mother's end had come.

Zhao Jiangsu, however, knew all about it. And why wouldn't he? He had been the one to find Elias lying on the road, bloodied and barely breathing, alongside the violated dead bodies of his parents. He knew everything that had happened but he had never let Elias know the extent to which his parents had actually suffered before being embraced by the mercy called death.

Elias saw as Zhao Jiangsu merely stared at him without saying a word. Tears shimmered in the old man's eyes and a few fell down his face. His wrinkled hands reached up and wiped those tears off slowly. At the age he was, and after everything he had been through, he no more felt the need to try to hide his sorrows or to decorate his grief. He had seen too much to want to pretend that the world was a good place.

He no longer believed that only smiles deserved to be seen and pain must be concealed. Elias put his hand on Zhao Jiangsu's arm. He wanted to show the old man that he was grateful to him – for listening to his story, for understanding his pain, and for sharing in the measureless grief of his parents' violent deaths. Until now, there had been no one in his life in the United States who he felt could come close to understanding the things he had been through.

You had to be a part of it, to have suffered through it, to have seen it with your own eyes to begin to comprehend what had unfolded in Nanking in 1937. To others, it was merely a story. To Elias and Zhao Jiangsu, it was their life marked by pain that still felt as sharp as a knife twisting in your guts.

Zhao Jiangsu looked at Elias and said, *"The darkness of the night always ends with dawn."*

Elias laughed with bitterness and said, *"Yes, for others. For me, there is just one long unending night."*

"Don't say that!" Zhao Jiangsu protested. *"You'll see things changing for you soon, Elias. Trust me on this if you don't want to trust fate."*

"There's still time to attend the group meeting I told you about. Do you still want to go?" Elias asked, referring to the Alcoholics Anonymous meeting.

Zhao Jiangsu still wanted to accompany him to the meeting. They went there and caught the end of it. Being there, Elias realised it might benefit him to be in a support group where people shared the same problem as him. It might even help him get rid of this habit that was now controlling him more than he wanted.

On the way back from the meeting, Elias thought he should give Zhao Jiangsu a taste of truly American food: a hamburger from one of his favourite joints in the city. He thought about the old man's health but decided that one burger wouldn't affect it too badly. The thoughts of Fei and Lois waiting at the department fled from their minds completely.

Elias drove to the drive-through of the restaurant and ordered two burgers.

"And they will give us our food right here, right now?" Zhao Jiangsu asked, his eyebrows raised in surprise. This practice of driving to a place, getting your food and eating it

on the go perhaps wasn't something that happened in China.

"Yes, Jiangsu tài. This is for when you want your food quickly and don't have the time to dine in," Elias explained happily. He felt quite pleased to introduce the old man to the quirks of the American culture which seemed to surprise him to no end.

"Let's see what they have whipped up for us in such little time. Where I come from, meals take time to prepare and then some more time to eat," Zhao Jiangsu said, unwrapping his burger as Elias stepped on the gas.

"Oh!" Zhao Jiangsu exclaimed on taking the first bite of his cheeseburger.

Elias turned to look at him, laughed and asked, *"What happened? Is this not to your liking?"*

"No, no. But this is exactly like our 'rou jia mo'. I remember ever since I was a child, this was one of my favourite foods to eat. This meat sandwich is really good, too!" Zhao Jiangsu explained.

Elias laughed at the peculiar way of describing the food. He didn't remember eating this as a child in China and had, in fact, only been introduced to it when he had come to the

US. He said, *"I'm glad you like it. It's one of my favourites, too."*

"Yes, it's all good. But, don't go eating it too much now, Elias," Zhao Jiangsu warned with a frown on his face. *"You see, Fei has told me how eating meat and too much greasy food isn't good for health. She doesn't even let me eat the things I want to, saying it would affect my heart."* He had started off as a concerned parent, but by the end of the sentence, he sounded more like a sullen child, displeased at missing out of his favourite food because of his daughter who acted more like his parent.

At the mention of Fei, Elias suddenly became interested. He said, *"Really, is Fei very particular about such things?"*

"Oh you have no idea! That girl won't let me rest. It's 'don't eat this' for good food and 'eat this' for bland ones. Then there are her medicines – I mean my medicines! She never forgets and never lets me forget them either!" Zhao Jiangsu burst out as though he had been holding in all these grievances for a long, long time. The old man actually looked relieved to have someone to complain to in the figure of Elias.

Elias laughed and laughed. He liked that Zhao Jiangsu had someone to take care of him in his old age. He was glad Fei was doing a great job at it. He was also quietly envious. The thought of his own father – who had never grown old, never reached the age where Elias would have to be the one taking care of him rather than the other way round – tugged at his heart. He didn't want to think of what-ifs but he couldn't help himself either.

Through his mind's eye he saw his parents surviving, being with him all the way to the present, being old but healthy and alive. To distract himself, he thought to ask Zhao Jiangsu some questions about his life as a Chinese officer during that horrible time of war.

"Do you think about it a lot, Jiangsu tài? The war?"

"Think about it? That's a strange question to ask!" Zhao Jiangsu laughed, trying quite apparently to divert the conversation to a safer topic.

"It's not strange at all. I want to know how you felt in the aftermath of the war that left the entire country in ruins. You were a soldier, you perhaps saw more than the civilians did. Then why do you not want to talk about it?" Elias replied.

"Because it's water under the bridge," Zhao Jiangsu said placidly.

"Is it, really?" Elias demanded.

"No," Zhao Jiangsu answered quietly.

"You can talk about it with me, Jiangsu tài. If you think I should talk about my past then what's stopping you from doing the same?" Elias questioned. As far as he saw it, this conversation should go both ways.

"Let me ask you something, Elias. In all that happened in your childhood, is there something that weighs heavy on your heart? Is there something that makes you blame yourself? What actually stops you from talking about it?" Zhao Jiangsu asked.

"Only the deep desire for secrecy. And the knowledge that no one would ever understand the things I have been through," Elias answered after a moment of thought. And this was true. He was a very isolated person who never shared his life's history with anyone. It was the sudden arrival of Zhao Jiangsu in his life that had made him talk of all that happened so many years ago. He didn't want the old man to keep it all bottled up like he had for so long.

"You never had something as strong as guilt weighing as much as a mountain on your shoulders, did you?" Zhao Jiangsu asked.

"Guilt? What do you mean?" Elias asked, taken aback. He hadn't expected Zhao Jiangsu to say such a thing.

"Guilt, my child. I have found there is nothing quite like guilt to choke you up for good," Zhao Jiangsu said.

Elias was more and more perplexed. What guilt was he talking about? He had been a soldier and to defend his country he must have had to take up arms. He couldn't possibly be referring to the guilt of serving his country by being in the army.

"I don't quite get what you mean," Elias said.

"For you to understand what I mean, I'll have to tell you of things about myself that I have never told anyone. Not even Fei, not even my wife. I guess I must have thought they would think less of me if I ever told them of all the things I did during the war...." Zhao Jiangsu said.

"You can tell me. I won't judge you for it," Elias said with sincerity.

Elias had done and seen enough in his life to know not to judge people for what they did when life made more demands on them than they were capable of justifying. As they say, desperate times call for desperate measures. Elias knew that moral lines often became blurred during wartime. Humans were pushed to the edge of their humanity and sanity. Oftentimes in war, people did things that they never would have thought they were capable of doing during times of peace.

"I did the worst thing I could have done at that time, Elias," Zhao Jiangsu said. He had suddenly started shivering. Elias reached out with his hand toward the old man and patted him on the shoulder, trying to give him the courage to let out all that he had kept in for years and years.

"What happened?" Elias asked gently.

"You must have heard stories of the things that happened during the war…I mean, even before the atrocities that happened in Nanking?" Zhao Jiangsu asked Elias.

"I did hear of the things that were happening in the country at the time. It's funny how much I know," Elias laughed, *"because my parents tried so hard to shield me*

knowing the horrors of the war tearing the country apart."

"How did you know if they didn't tell you?" Zhao Jiangsu wanted to know.

"Oh the children always have their ways. Only one of us had to put his ear to the door when the elders were talking. If one knew it meant every single one of us knew. Even the old grannies wouldn't share information with the speed of children. I can tell you that those were mere horror stories to us, though. We were scared but also secretly thrilled at tales of such danger. All of us wanted to be soldiers so we could fight and protect our people. That's just how a child thinks. Later, when we actually underwent the horrors ourselves, we realised how fragile human lives really are..." Elias explained.

"Yes, all young boys want to be soldiers. It was one of my biggest dreams too, when I was young. I wanted to be a hero, a saviour. I wanted people to point their fingers at me with adulation and tell stories of how I had saved lives," Zhao Jiangsu said with regret tingling his voice.

"That's pretty close to what I wanted at the time," Elias agreed. *"Yet I knew my parents abhorred violence in any and*

all forms. I knew they were so proud of my musical skills. Even as I wanted to be a soldier I always knew I'd be a violinist. To make them happy."

"That's a noble thing to do, Elias, wanting to make your parents happy."

"So what did you do?" Elias pressed, noticing that the conversation might soon slip away from the main point.

"I abandoned the army at Nanking," Zhao Jiangsu said abruptly.

"As many other Chinese soldiers did," Elias answered after a moment of pause.

"That does not condone my crime of absconding from the army when my services were needed the most," Zhao Jiangsu said tiredly. He looked older, much older than his age as he confessed to the crime that had been haunting him for a very long time. At the same time, he looked lighter – as if some invisible weight had been lifted off of him. It was strange but it was obvious to Elias's eyes. The confession made him feel lighter, no doubt.

"Why did you abandon the army then?" Elias asked. He knew if he wanted Zhao Jiangsu to process the trauma that

his time in the army had left on him, he needed to make him talk about it.

"It was a hopeless situation. There was fighting, endless fighting. I could remember no past and could see no future. The only images in my head – even when I slept – were of war. Dead and broken bodies, bloodied and torn limbs, guts spilling out. You have no idea of the things I saw," Zhao Jiangsu said, rubbing his hands all over his face as if doing so would wipe out the picture of ruin and gore from his memories.

"I can imagine. I saw some of those things, too," Elias said sympathetically.

"Yes but when you are in the army, you just feel responsible for it. When your people die right in front of your eyes you feel as if their blood is on your hands, though you never raised a weapon against them," he said.

"Weren't you in the Nanking Garrison Force, Jiangsu tài?" Elias recalled.

"Yes. I will be the first person to admit that we were not prepared for the war. The army was weakened from fighting in Shanghai. Instead of being belligerent, we were *retreating. The Japanese had started their incessant shelling and aerial bombing. So many times we just felt like fish in a barrel waiting to be shot. What were we but fodder for the Japanese war machinery?"* Zhao Jiangsu mused.

"Is that how the army felt?" Elias asked.

"Yes, the morale was really down. And we were so disorganised. We didn't even know where to regroup. So many of my fellow soldiers were wounded and then died of injuries they sustained from fragments of bombs and shrapnel. The truth is, our division that was assigned to protect Nanking was not at its full strength."

"But I have read that the commander issued the order to evacuate the city," Elias said.

"That order was given, yes. But I deserted the army before the official order was given. When the final assault on the city happened, I had already decided to give up fighting. We were so desperate to leave, to survive if we could..." Zhao Jiangsu drew a deep, shaky breath.

"But you were not able to get out of the city," Elias stated.

"No, I wasn't. The main escape route for us was to go over the Yangtze River, which lay to the east of Nanking. But

the Japanese very smartly cut off that route. They advanced on us from that side so all roads were blocked for us," Zhao Jiangsu said.

"One would think that with the stone walls of the city, it'd have been harder for the Japanese to conquer it," Elias commented.

"Even those stone walls stood no chance against the unrelenting force of the Japanese army. Though all the gates leading into the city were closed and barricade, and we also bolstered up the protection using concrete and sandbags, in the end it all amounted to nothing. The city fell," Zhao Jiangsu said with despair that still lingered in his voice after so many years.

"Nothing worked against them?" Elias persisted though he obviously knew the answer through history.

"Nothing. Not the trenches, not the barbed wires, not the moats, not the minefields. Not even the mountains could prevent the city from falling," Zhao Jiangsu said.

"Weren't there more soldiers called into service? Common young men who were no soldiers?" Elias questioned.

"Yes, those poor young men were recruited to build up the army's strength. But they had no training. Even people like me, who had training, lost the will to fight. I don't know what made those young boys sign up to pay with their lives. You know the Japanese did not spare the soldiers at all," Zhao Jiangsu explained.

"It was as if destruction was fated," Elias expressed in a resigned voice.

"Yes. Though there were some idealistic young soldiers who pledged to die together protecting the city, there were many like me – cynical one, hopeless ones. We were older and completely cured of all such idealistic thoughts."

"You already know it would have made little difference had you stayed behind in the army," Elias said.

"It wouldn't perhaps have made any difference. Yet I know if I had stayed my conscience would be clear. I could have remained and fought. There were so many soldiers who did their best though their fellows were chopped to pieces by the artillery fire. They kept fighting till their last breath. In that, there is honour," Zhao Jiangsu said, conviction making his voice tremble.

"Some might call it honour, some might say it is stupidity," Elias remarked. The way he saw it, Zhao Jiangsu had displayed only the most human of weaknesses in Nanking. The survival instinct was so strong in human beings. When it came down to avoiding certain death, there were no other choices other than ones like the old man had made.

"It was only later that I realised that I should never have deserted. I should have fought until I died. An honourable death is better than a lifetime of guilt," Zhao Jiangsu countered.

"Is it?" Elias asked. He wasn't too sure of that.

"Yes. Yes, it is. Life is not just a matter of flesh and blood. Things like bravery and valour, heroism and nobility – they really do exist. And I had the chance to prove I had those qualities. Yet I gave it up. I ran away like a frightened little dog with its tail between its legs," Zhao Jiangsu said with brutal honesty.

"Don't say that," Elias objected. It hurt him to listen to the old man describe himself in such terms that reeked of self-loathing. He was actually shocked to see that the self-

blame had persisted over the decades. In truth, Zhao Jiangsu was one of the bravest men Elias had ever known. And then to have him speak of himself in such terms – it upset him more than anything the old man had said until now.

"That is how I thought of myself from the time that I deserted to the time that I tried putting things to right," Zhao Jiangsu said.

"How did you put things to right?" Elias asked, having no doubt whatsoever that the old man must have made up for what he saw as his biggest weakness.

"Through you," Zhao Jiangsu said.

"Through me?" Elias echoed. He thought about it for a minute; things were starting to make sense to him now. A full picture was emerging. He could see where the old man was going with it. So he wasn't shocked when the old man answered,

"It was through saving you that I absolved my guilt – or tried to. Do you want to listen to all that happened?"

Elias nodded. It was about time that he knew the whole story.

Chapter 10
Fight Or Flight

"There was a river of blood on the street."

"My father's." It wasn't a question but a statement – an unflinching look at what had happened.

Zhao Jiangsu jerked his head, as if still trying but failing to turn his face away from all that his eyes had seen that fateful morning. He stared straight ahead, still unable to wipe out the image of horror, the likes of which no one could imagine. He saw the beheaded body of the young Russian man; his torso thrown to one side while his head topped by a thinning reddish mop lay on the other.

The wide-open blue eyes stared at the sky, as if questioning God in death. Zhao Jiangsu had walked a few steps forward in the direction of the small body of the little boy, who he knew was the beheaded man's son. Without looking at the child from a close range, Zhao Jiangsu deemed him as dead as his father; his body did not writhe in pain nor did he seem to be breathing. There was a small pool of blood around the child's body with its arm bent out of shape. Zhao

Jiangsu barely managed to swallow the bile that rose in his throat at this sight. For some reason, the broken arm of the son had made him feel sicker than the sight of the decapitated head of the father. It was just the senseless cruelty of it. *'To murder the child and then break his arm, too? You had to be completely devoid of all humanity to desecrate the dead body of a child,'* Zhao Jiangsu had thought in those few moments.

"But what about my mother?" Elias's voice came to Zhao Jiangsu, as though from a far off tunnel. He had been sucked into the now-familiar void of the past. He turned toward Elias in the car – once more taken aback at his miraculous survival – and look at him with confusion.

"I asked about my mother, Jiangsu tài. I know she died but in what state did you find her?" Elias looked at the old man with a piercing stare, as if willing him to give it to him straight, to not spare him as he'd always suspected the old man of doing.

"When I found her, she was still breathing," Zhao Jiangsu finally told Elias the thing he'd always hidden from him. Elias was struck dumb by this revelation. He had always assumed that his mother had died along with his father. For some reason, he had believed that.

Perhaps this was owing to the fact that in his mind, his mother and father were inseparable: he could never imagine the one existing without the other. So to now find that his mother had outlived his father, even if for a few hours, stunned him. At the back of his mind, he was slowly realising that he had perfected this fiction of both his parents falling dead at the same time as a way to defend himself from the awful reality.

He had learned later how the Japanese forces had dealt with women during the fall of the city. He had a clear idea of what must have transpired. He understood now that to protect his sanity, he had repressed the gruesome knowledge. Denying the most likely possibility, he had told himself his mother was killed by the same blow that had ended his father.

But now, he recalled everything.

It was as if the wrecks of his memory were being pulled out of the dark sea of self-imposed forgetfulness. The picture was becoming clear in his mind. He remembered his father being beheaded by a bayonet. He recalled running to his father, screaming like a wounded animal. He remembered being snatched by the Japanese soldier who threw him down to the ground and the oblivion that followed. But now, he also remembered the crucial detail he had disremembered: that his mother was running to him as he had been bayoneted. In fact, the last image he had before the darkness was of his mother's face. He could no longer tell himself self-crafted lie he had always believed in. It was time to know the truth.

"She was alive?" he rasped.

Zhao Jiangsu nodded, calculating in his mind how much to reveal to Elias.

He knew he couldn't tell him all the brutality that had been inflicted upon his mother. He just couldn't. The sight of the young woman with her clothes ripped off, her body torn and bleeding, had never left him. What he was still haunted by the most was her silence. Even in this state of agony, the woman had not cried out.

It was as if the night's horror had taken away her power of speech. She had just lain on the dusty road, her body bleeding and her eyes wide open. Zhao Jiangsu had assumed her dead, too, and she was as good as. He had approached her body to cover it with her torn clothes that were thrown to the side and that's when he had seen her blinking. He had jumped back in horror.

"Miss? Miss?" Zhao Jiangsu had said to her.

The woman had taken in a few painful breaths. Her mouth and eyes were badly bruised, as though the soldiers had punched and clawed at her numerous times. As Zhao Jiangsu had uncomfortably tried to cover her, she had said just one word: *"Elias."*

Zhao Jiangsu had looked at her then and she had said the name again, barely managing to nod in the direction of her son. Understanding what she wanted him to do, Zhao Jiangsu had walked over to the child's body, only fulfilling her wish, sure that the child was not alive.

He had turned the child's body to face him and had seen that he had been bayoneted in the stomach. Somehow, though, Zhao Jiangsu had seen, the weapon had not pierced the child's abdomen. It had grazed his skin and had torn off a patch of skin. That was what the blood was from. The child was still breathing. He had turned to the mother to inform her but saw that her eyes were closed. He had put the child back gently on the road and walked over to the mother.

She was dead. It was as if she had been holding out but barely, waiting for someone to come along and take responsibility that she no longer could for her child. As soon as she had seen that happen, her last breath had left her body.

Zhao Jiangsu had done the only thing he could. He had pulled the bodies of the parents to the side and had covered them as best as he could. He had no time to bury them. He had to save their child. He had pulled the little boy up in his arms, careful of his injury. At the last moment, his eyes had roamed over to the violin case and he had picked it up as well. *'The child will need something to remember his parents by,'* he had thought.

"Jiangsu tài? What happened to my mother?" Elias asked again, watching the old man go in and out his past memories.

"She was raped," said Zhao Jiangsu bluntly. There was no reason for him to lie to Elias who must already know what fate had awaited most women in Nanking.

Elias sat quietly, taking his time to process the words that the older man had said so directly to him. It was like ripping off the bandage all at once, and exposing the wound which, though no longer festered, still throbbed with the ghost of its former pain.

"She died within minutes," Zhao Jiangsu said, deciding to keep all the details to himself.

"Her death came swiftly. The only thing she said to me – her last words, Elias – was your name. She wanted me to go to you, to make sure you lived. As soon as she saw me assume responsibility for you, she died. I believe she was clinging to her last breaths just to make certain that you will be taken care of when she was gone."

Tears welled up in Elias's eyes. The knowledge that his mother had died so brutally, so violently, raged like wildfire in his blood. He gripped the steering wheel of his car tightly till his knuckles turned white. Then he took a few deep breaths and released his grip, as Zhao Jiangsu watched him quietly, giving him the time to come to terms with his ancient grief that had always remained fresh.

When Elias spoke, his voice was rough like sandpaper. He said, *"You had already turned away from the army by then?"*

Zhao Jiangsu nodded his head. *"You might not remember, but I had been to your house the night before. Your family was leaving the hut for the safety zone, as your father told me. The hut was dark and it was night. I remember how people used to extinguish all lamps in those days, just to give the Japanese the idea that there was no one living for them to slaughter there."*

"I remember that the night we left two badly injured soldiers came to our house, asking for a place to stay," Elias recalled. He remembered the words of horror the soldiers had said and the worry it had provoked on his father's already weary face.

Most of all, he recalled the very bad state one of the two soldiers was in. He was still talking but his words were slurred, as though he was drunk. Now that Elias thought about it, he could see the torn, dusty and blood-smeared uniform. Maybe he imagined those details, since it was too dark for him to actually see this, but that was how it was supposed to look.

"Yes, that was me and my fellow soldier Wen Jiashou."

"You remember my father, then?" Elias's eyes lit up at the thought. There was no one alive who knew his father, even as briefly as Zhao Jiangsu had known him.

"Yes, I remember him well, my child. He was a good man with a good heart. I could see it in the way he worried about his family. He lent us the room to stay, when so many before had turned us away because they were rightly worried about the consequences."

"What consequences?"

"Of harbouring Chinese soldiers. The Japanese army did not spare my brethren, Elias. Nor did they deal lightly with anyone who was found to have sympathised with them."

"My father had seen a lifetime of war, Jiangsu tài. Perhaps that's what made him so compassionate. Above all, though, he was a family man. My mother and I came first to him. In my life, I saw him struggle to keep us safe and happy. He always did that. I am relieved to know that he died without knowing what befell my mother after him."

A few moments of quiet hung in the air. The painful past intruded and then filled the atmosphere of the car so that the two occupants felt they were no longer in America but back in those old streets suffused with the sight and smell of death. A honking car that whooshed past them on the road brought them back to the present.

Elias cleared his throat and said, *"Please tell me more about how you left the army."*

"Do you really want to know this and not what happened after I found you?" Zhao Jiangsu asked, surprised. He had expected Elias to forget about his less-than-illustrious streak in the army.

"Yes. You can tell me about that later, after I have recovered a little. Meanwhile, I want to know the things that you experienced," Elias said, turning to look at the old man. There was a directness in Elias's eyes that told the old man he was really interested in hearing what he had to say.

Though he did not show it, Zhao Jiangsu was taken aback by the sincerity in Elias's words. The younger man perhaps didn't realise it but he was displaying a true spirit of generosity by lending a listening ear to a man who had gone his entire like without talking.

"Well, it is a long story…" Zhao Jiangsu began.

"I have time to hear," Elias interrupted. Then he motioned the old man to continue while he gave him his full attention.

"Where should I start?"

"How about you start at the beginning? The time that you were on the frontline, defending the city of Nanking?"

"Yes, I will have to go all the way back…" Zhao Jiangsu said, settling back in his seat. His eyes became unfocused as the present world vanished…and was replaced by the unforgiving past.

***

The stuttering sound of the machine guns reverberated in the night air. As the front line of the army took a breather and fell back, they saw the sparks in the air and heard the loud incomprehensible taunt that came from the other side.

Zhao Jiangsu felt a deep sense of frustration as he walked back to the temporary camp they had set up. He rubbed his eyes and said a few cuss words under his breath. In truth, he no longer knew how to keep going. The city, despite its ancient walls, seemed so indefensible. The topography gave the attackers a distinct advantage.

The Yangtze River behind the city was also a problem because it choked off escape for the defending army. Then there were the contradictory instructions that the soldiers received from the commanders in charge. While one had asked them to fight to the last man, the other only wanted to use delay tactics for the occupation that seemed inevitable.

"They moved the capital to Chongqing," one soldier remarked. He was a middle-aged man with a sparse beard and red-rimmed eyes.

"Yes. The young ones don't understand it but to me it is a signal for impending defeat," Zhao Jiangsu had answered wearily. He had looked at the conscripted soldiers and even the young ones who had voluntarily signed up in the army.

He recalled how enthusiastically every single one of them had played their part in boosting up the city's defence. The stone walls that were constructed around the city were all bolstered with machine gun installations and layers of sandbags. They had closed all six gates to the city and had also added up a concrete defensive layer to keep out the intruders. Then there was also the Fukuo Line, which was really just a web of minefields, barbed wires and trenches, which was to serve as the final defence of the city.

Zhao Jiangsu knew how sorely demoralised the army really was. After being defeated at the Battle of Shanghai, it was no wonder that the soldiers felt like they could do nothing to save the city. Then, there was the continuous aerial bombing by the Japanese air force which never left them in peace. Zhao Jiangsu felt resigned to death that he only hoped would come swiftly when it did come for him. During all this time, it was only the thoughts of his family that kept him going. When he closed his eyes, he saw the faces of his little daughter and his wife, and he felt a deep yearning to go back to them.

Zhao Jiangsu's last fight in the city was near the peaks of Zijinshan Mountain. A small group of soldiers had encamped there to protect the city and its historical sites, Zhao Jiangsu included. He remembered how stealthily the Japanese forces had approached their small encampment. Even as the commander had yelled his instruction to fall back, the attack had begun in earnest. He remembered the shelling, and his fellows unable to cope because of being taken by surprise. His companion Wen Jiashou had been shot. He did not know what else to do so he had wrapped a torn piece of cloth around his wound, hoping to stem the flow of blood. Then, watching the others being chopped one by one, he had tried saving the one life he could. He had pulled Wen Jiashou on his back and had run down the other side of the mountain while the forces were busy killing off the other soldiers. He did this without thought, almost on instinct. The only thought in his mind was how he had to survive because other lives depended on him.

The Japanese soldiers did not notice him retreating. This was not something that Zhao Jiangsu was proud of but he saw it as a necessity. The bloodcurdling screams of his fellow soldiers, their bloodied bodies were all the images that he knew he'd carry with him to the day he'd die. Taking Wen Jiashou down the mountain, he had run down the dark narrow alleys of the city below to find accommodation.

His friend needed to rest. He didn't turn back to see who had made it and who hadn't. This was the time when it was every man for himself. Even so, he couldn't bear to leave Wen Jiashou behind. Running from door to door, he had asked a few people to let them in. However, he saw their predicament. He knew he'd be putting their lives in danger because he understood full well what would happen to them if they were found sheltering soldiers.

So he had gone on until a young man, who didn't look Chinese, had allowed him inside his home. He had taken the first easy breath in hours inside that house where he had come across the little boy who was now sitting beside him in the car.

***

"This was my house," Elias said.

"Yes, your house," Zhao Jiangsu confirmed, emerging out of the sea of past memories.

"What happened to your friend, Jiangsu tài? Did he not survive?" Elias asked with compassion in his voice.

"He died in my arms," Zhao Jiangsu said. It was obvious he still mourned his dead friend whose life he had been unable to save.

"But he was able to talk when he was in our house," Elias said.

"He did talk. Well, our Wen was a talker," Zhao Jiangsu laughed fondly. *"But that was nothing more than the last burst of energy before the inevitable death. He lost too much blood. You know what the night was like. I couldn't have*

transported him to one of the city's hospitals if I had tired."

"Was he in a lot of pain?" Elias asked with sympathy in his eyes.

"Yes, he was. Even so, he did not make a fuss, he did not cry out. At one point in the night, he just closed his eyes and died, as if he were falling asleep. That was Wen for you. He never protested, he never grumbled. I guess you could say he was not like me. He took death as uncomplainingly as he had taken the violence of the army. I knew he was dead, though. When you have been a soldier this long, you become as familiar with death as if it were a lifelong friend, or a shadow if you will."

"Then what did you do?"

"Then? I closed his eyes and allowed him his rest. When it neared dawn, I said my last goodbyes to him. I was sorry I couldn't do any more for him. I wish I could have saved him. Just another life that was lost to the war, eh?"

"No," Elias shook his head, *"he was a person who died. He died protecting us. For that, he is an honourable man."*

With tears in his eyes, Zhao Jiangsu said, *"Yes, that he was. I am so happy that you acknowledge that, Elias.*

Otherwise, people just count dead soldiers as mere figures, just one of the numbers of the casualties of war. For them, soldiers sign up to die."

"*No one is just a number, Jiangsu tài. Even soldiers. They are humans with dreams and fear, love and hate."*

Zhao Jiangsu could only nod. There were no words to explain how understood he felt in those few moments.

"*Then in the morning you found me?"*

"*Yes, right there on the streets."*

"*What made you want to run down that mountain with your friend, Jiangsu tài? What was it that propelled you to save your life?"* Elias asked.

"*I don't know what. But I just know that there was one thought in my mind: Fei."*

"*Your daughter."*

"*Yes, my daughter. I only thought of how my daughter would be left fatherless. I was one of many soldiers in the army, Elias, but the only father my daughter had. I couldn't leave her and her mother to fend for themselves in the cruel world."*

"And do you think they would have made it, that they would have survived, if not for you?" Elias prompted.

"No, I doubt it. It took a lot of effort to get them safely out of the mainland. Women, even little girls, were not safe in the country at the time. I think they needed me to make it out alive."

"So why then do you regret your decision? The way I see it, you saved the lives of your wife and your daughter. And mine, for that matter."

Zhao Jiangsu was taken aback. He had not thought about it in this way at all. All this time, he had been shouldering the guilt of abandoning the army at Nanking. He had thought they needed him the most. But after what Elias had said, he was starting to look at things differently.

Perhaps the army had not needed him as badly as his family had, after all. Perhaps the army was already fighting a losing battle and to have saved the lives of his family in the bargain by leaving the army…perhaps that redeemed him. Saving this thought to think about it later, he turned to Elias and said, *"It was on the next morning that I found you."*

Elias nodded and said, *"On the streets, with my parents."*

"Yes. That was the time I had decided to head to the safety zone. There had been rumours that we had heard before, that the safety zones might also shelter soldiers."

"And you decided to take me with you," Elias said.

"Yes. I did. That was the day that I decided it was my responsibility to do what I could to save your life."

Elias smiled at the old man in gratefulness. This was an entirely new aspect of this story and he wanted to know how things had proceeded from thereon before he had regained consciousness.

Chapter 11
A Life of Strife

"I was in a pretty bad way, wasn't I?" Elias asked, shaking his head. He still had the long scar on his stomach that forever reminded him of that horrible night. Try as he might, he couldn't forget.

"You had lost blood. You were unconscious. Or maybe it was the shock that made it worse. You looked lifeless to me, Elias," Zhao Jiangsu confirmed. *"You were as pale as a ghost. I know I'd have left you for dead if it wasn't for your mother who urged me to check if you were fine."*

"That's what my mother was like. Always thinking of me. Even as she was dying, she thought only of me…" Elias said, swallowing hard. He didn't want tears to flow from his eyes. He was afraid if he started crying over his mother he might not stop for a very long time.

Clearing his throat, he added, *"Then what did you do? Please excuse my poor recall – seeing as I was not awake, I can't remember anything that happened."* He smiled weakly, acknowledging his feeble attempt to lighten the situation.

Zhao Jiangsu said, *"What could I do? I picked you up like a sack of potato and marched on."*

"Like a sack of potato?" Elias's eyes widened.

"Well, not really. You were injured, remember. I actually carried you in my arms quite gently that day. You were a small boy, small for your age. Anyway, since that isn't a very soldierly thing to do, I prefer to say it the way I did," Zhao Jiangsu stuck his nose in the air.

"All right!" Elias answered, pressing his lips together to conceal his smile. The old man and his old ways! It was quite amusing to watch how he held on to his own personal code of behaviour, based on his military training, in all situations.

"So like a sack of potato," Zhao Jiangsu emphasised with a nod, *"I carted you through the deserted streets of Nanking. It was a good thing that some foreigners had stayed behind to establish the safety zones. Or I have no idea where we'd be."*

"Maybe then even the few who survived wouldn't have," Elias said. He had read later of the casualties of the Rape of Nanking. He was convinced there were fewer wars in human

history that could rival this one for its utter inhumanity and cruelty.

"That is for sure. You do know that the safety zone did not allow Chinese soldiers to take refuge there?" Zhao Jiangsu asked, turning to look Elias in the eyes.

"They weren't?" Elias asked, taken aback. He had not been aware of this rule. *"Then how were you able to get in?"*

"By pretending to be a civilian. I had already changed out of my uniform. It was your father who gave me his clothes to wear."

"He did?" Elias asked.

"Yes, before he left the house to me and Wen. He was kind enough to lend the both of us a pair of his trousers and shirts. He knew that we wouldn't be able to make it very far, dressed as we were in our soldier's uniform. Though your father was taller than me, I put on his clothes. I had to stay alive and if that meant rolling up the ends of my trousers then so be it," Zhao Jiangsu said.

"Wen never got to use his," Elias said regretfully.

"No, he didn't," the old man said with a grave look on his face.

Elias cleared his throat and asked, *"Then what happened?"* He wanted to know but at the same time, he was scared of knowing the truth.

"Then…" Zhao Jiangsu said, his voice sounding as remote as if he were speaking from the other end of a dark tunnel, *"Then began one of the toughest journeys of my life. The one where I had to save not just myself but you."*

Elias remained quiet, waiting for the old man to grab his hand and walk him back in time.

***

The roads were deserted. Though it was winter, Zhao Jiangsu was sweating through his clothes. One of his arms was around the young boy's legs, fastening him in place. With the other, he wiped his brow.

The boy wasn't too heavy and it wasn't particularly hard to carry him over his shoulder. He knew he was perspiring out of fear. He had been keeping to the small, narrow alleyways but you never know where the Japanese soldiers might be lurking in wait.

He would have no chance of escape with the young boy's responsibility on him. For that reason, it was all the more crucial for him to play it safe. It seemed to him that the earth was exerting more gravity on him than ever before.

"Elias," Zhao Jiangsu repeated the name under his breath. It tasted strange to him, this name. So foreign, so new. This boy with sharp cheekbones and a long straight nose seemed foreign to him even with his eyes closed. The curly hair with glints of copper in it – much like his dead father – also screamed of his foreignness. *"Perhaps that might save him,"* Zhao Jiangsu thought with forced optimism.

Zhao Jiangsu craned his neck out of the narrow side alley he was in to check if Japanese forces were around or not. There was the main street across which there were more narrow alleys that twisted like a maze and led to the old neighbourhood of the city.

This main street was developed a few years ago and was wide and clear. It offered no hiding spot, however. Those old alleys on the other side, though – they were the ones he could easily lose himself in. No Japanese soldier would be able to trace him once he got to the other side. He knew he'd be able to reach the area where the US Embassy in the city was located pretty quickly once he got to the other side. Just as he was about to dash out on the street, he heard the unmistakable sound of carousing men. There were loud cheers and hoots and the sound of drunken footsteps that were confused as to where they wanted to head.

He peeked out furtively and saw that there indeed was a troop of Japanese soldiers walking down the road. *"Look at them strutting around, as if they owned our country,"* Zhao Jiangsu said, spitting on the wall to his right. He was enraged but there was little else he could do. He quickly retreated and walked down a few doors before entering an abandoned house.

The place looked perfectly preserved, as if its owners had just gone out for a walk and would be back any minute. They must have left in a hurry, leaving everything they had owned behind. It was a modest-sized house but was tastefully furnished. Zhao Jiangsu left the main door open so as to give the illusion that there was no one hiding inside. He walked to the top floor of the two-story house and entered the last room at the end of the corridor. He lay the boy's unmoving body on the bed and then walked over to the window.

He opened the curtains a little and peeked out. From this angle, he could spot the approach of the Japanese soldiers.

Hours passed. No one came. Behind him, he could hear the shallow breathing of the boy who had still not woken up from his slumber. *"And when he opens his eyes he'll know all his family is gone and he's alone in the world,"* Zhao Jiangsu thought, running his hand over the boy's forehead. Elias was running a fever now.

He knew he couldn't wait too long for the boy to receive medical treatment. For his part, he had lived a rough life in the army. He preferred for his wounds to heal of their own accord than put any effort into the task. For this young boy, though, things were different. He looked so fragile, so unbearably innocent that he brought out all of Zhao Jiangsu's fatherly instincts. Plus, Elias seemed to be around his daughter Fei's age which made him all the more protective of him.

As it turned out, Zhao Jiangsu had to wait until nightfall before heading out of the house again. He knew he had to be careful; there was more than his own life at risk here. He picked Elias up in his arms again and went back to the corner of the alley, closing the door of the house gently behind him.

This time there were no Japanese soldiers and he successfully made it to the other side of the main street. He walked through the narrow alleys that wound into each other and perplexed even him in the congealing darkness that seemed to choke all air off. Zhao Jiangsu took deep breaths and carried on. He was an expert, though, and was out the other side before morning came. It was easy enough to get to the safety zone from there.

Zhao Jiangsu was stopped at the entrance of the safety zone by two guards who carried batons. *'As if these batons would stop any intruder,'* Zhao Jiangsu thought sarcastically. He was carrying the boy who was now breathing shallowly and the guards saw that. Without much ado, they let him in. He had started to fear that Elias wouldn't make it.

Once inside the safety zone, he was approached by a German man who was the supervisor of this safety zone. He had a wide face and ruddy cheeks and thinning blond hair. He introduced himself as Herr Adalwen and reassured Zhao Jiangsu that he and his son would be safe here. He waved his large hands about and directed them to head towards one small building around which there were several small tents pitched in a circle. After a quick count, Zhao Jiangsu concluded there had to be about twenty to twenty-five such tents. They weren't too big but they seemed already to be crammed with people who had fled for their lives. The man called Adalwen did not investigate the history of the two males, Zhao Jiangsu was relieved to see. He had just assumed Elias was his son or a relative, though the two hardly looked alike.

Zhao Jiangsu did not correct him for he knew that would work in both his own and Elias's favour. For his part, he did not reveal that he was a disarmed soldier to the authorities. Though he knew under the law a disarmed soldier was granted protection, he also knew the Japanese military would honour no law. So yes, he practised deceit and pretended to be a civilian.

Medical aid was soon given to Elias. All through the night, Zhao Jiangsu kept vigil beside the boy who now thrashed in his unconscious state, calling for his mother. He lay his cool palm on Elias's burning forehead and hoped the fever would come down. When dawn broke, thankfully the fever did too. Elias was breathing deeply now, and the nurse reassured him that his 'son' would regain consciousness soon. Herr Adalwen visited them once more during the course of the night. He asked, *"Have you any rations or clothes with you?"*

Zhao Jiangsu looked at him blankly. As of now, he only had the clothes on his back and even those weren't his own. He cleared his throat and with considerable embarrassment answered, *"No, I don't."*

"Oh that's all right," Adalwen said magnanimously. *"We do encourage civilians to bring with them all the supplies that they could, seeing as we are running low on them ourselves. However, it is fine if you didn't bring anything. I am sure you had to leave everything back home when you made a run for your life."*

Once more, Zhao Jiangsu let him assume. He only nodded his head and then said, *"How are the other people doing here in the safety zone?"*

"Poorly. We try to provide as many basic provisions as we could but the influx is a lot more than we are equipped to handle here. Then we also have to fight off the Japanese soldiers every day. They are convinced we are harbouring Chinese soldiers here and every day they come looking."

Zhao Jiangsu gulped. He curled his fingers into a tight fist lest he blurted out the secret that he, too, was a soldier merely pretending to not be one. When he spoke, the words that came out were: *"What do you mean? I thought everybody was safe here...."*

"Well, ideally, everyone should be safe. But we have to admit, our first priority are the citizens. When it comes to soldiers, we can do little to protect them, though we are trying to convince the top rank of the Japanese military to allow the soldiers some reprieve."

"What have they been doing to soldiers, the Japanese?"

"We have heard very bad news. One of the groups that made it alive here reported seeing the entire river Yangtze choking with the dead bodies of soldiers. This clearly means the Japanese forces are hell-bent on killing off every man that has a weapon."

"Is no one offering any resistance?"

The German shook his head and said, *"Everyone seems to have given up. Though the Chinese in the city far outnumber the Japanese soldiers, it seems that they have admitted defeat. So far as we have heard, there are no insurgencies sprouting here. People have decided to keep their heads down with the hopes that that would ensure their survival."*

"And does it? Are the civilians being let off by the Japanese?" Zhao Jiangsu asked, knowing full well the answer to that question. He had seen with his own eyes the slashed bodies, the smashed in windows, the looted houses and the raped women left to die.

Adalwen hung his head for a moment, as if weighed down by the horrible reality. Then he looked at him with dread written on his face, *"No, they are not. So many here have described their ordeal to us. One woman made it to the safety zone just last morning. She was bleeding and was badly injured. She told us how she had been raped by the Japanese soldiers who broke into her house. Two of her female relatives were taken away by the same soldiers. She was frantic because she didn't know if those girls were even alive anymore."*

There was no suitable response to this but silence.

Adalwen continued, *"You'd think the Japanese would steer clear of any foreign residents of the city but no. So many Americans who live around here have reported incidents of looting and vandalism. One old lady Miss Mary lives on the Chien Ying Hsiang. She said two Japanese soldiers broke into her house, and took her china as well as the food she had saved in her house to donate to the safety zone."*

"There is just no end to what the enemy would do to us, is there?" Zhao Jiangsu said.

"None," Adalwen agreed.

"Have any soldiers also taken refuge here?" Zhao Jiangsu enquired.

"Yes, as a matter of fact. We asked the Chinese disarmed soldiers to assemble at that building there," Adalwen waved out the window where at a distance of a few meters Zhao Jiangsu could see the silhouette of a large building. *"We just asked them to separate from the civilians. It really would do no good to put the lives of both groups in danger. Anyway, they agreed so there they are, quarantined in that building."*

Zhao Jiangsu nodded, unconvinced of the usefulness of this plan. The way he saw it, the Japanese would attack whomever they deemed worthy of being attacked and while they did hate Chinese soldiers more, it was obvious they wouldn't stop at hurting civilians either. The violence that they handed out was indiscriminate like that.

Adalwen continued, *"The Japanese have not tried to enter the safety zone but for the past two days, there has been intermittent shelling."*

"They have fired at the camps here?" Zhao Jiangsu asked, surprised. He had been labouring under the illusion that until now the safety zone was safe from such obvious acts of violence.

"Yes. We heard multiple barrages of machine-gun fire. And when we rushed out to the camps, several people there were injured by the shelling."

Adalwen left after providing this overview of the city's conditions. Zhao Jiangsu sighed deeply and waited for the night to pass. When Elias fidgeted in his dreams, he held the young boy's small hand, hoping to convey to him that he wasn't alone, that he was there by his side to protect him.

When morning came, Zhao Jiangsu saw with his own eyes the terrible fate that befell the soldiers that had been confined to the building.

It was before midday that the Japanese came knocking at the entrance of the safety zone. With a flimsy pretext, they barged in and demanded that the soldiers be handed over to them. Before they headed to the building the soldiers were in, they marched along with the site of the camps, pretending to smoke out any soldiers that may be hiding in there but really just taking it as another chance of looting the refugees gathered there. Several sacks of food and other belongings were confiscated by the Japanese who then headed toward the building. A heavy silence hung in the air which was already thick with the sense of impending doom.

Zhao Jiangsu watched from the window of the makeshift hospital building as the soldiers were led out. The small group of Japanese soldiers herded out the Chinese soldiers which numbered at least four to five hundred. All their hands were tied behind their back. They were commanded out of the safety zone. Apparently, they weren't taken very far before they met their fate.

Zhao Jiangsu listened to the rapid stuttering of the machine guns. Underneath the noise, he could discern the last screams of agony of men that were his fellow soldiers. He felt a crushing sense of guilt – at having survived, at still being able to breathe when they were not. He wanted to cry but couldn't. He didn't feel he was worthy of even shedding tears. He just held the little boy Elias's delicate hand and waited for him to open his eyes. There was little else for him to do, no other person to save but him.

When Elias finally awoke after almost 14 hours since Zhao Jiangsu had brought him to the safety zone, he started immediately to call out for his parents.

"*Mǔqīn, mǔqīn!*" Elias cried. He seemed to have little recollection of what had happened to his parents.

Zhao Jiangsu ran his hand over the boy's head and asked him to breathe. He then explained, *"Your mother and father are not here."*

At this, Elias began to weep. He slid back down on the pillow and refused to talk anymore. A few days passed and the child remained mum. He did not say a word, he did not even ask for his parents any longer. Quietly, without anyone explaining the truth to him in its gory details, he seemed to have accepted the truth. Zhao Jiangsu was somewhat relieved because he didn't quite have the words to tell the little boy that his parents were no more.

He still spent most hours of the day by the side of the little boy who was slowly regaining his health. The wound on his stomach, thankfully, had not become infected and so the fever never came back. He began to eat slowly and colour returned to his cheeks. Zhao Jiangsu marvelled at the survival instinct and natural recovery process of the child, forgetting the fact that some wounds were invisible and ran deeper than the eye could perceive.

The day Zhao Jiangsu handed back the violin he had retrieved from the sight of the massacre of his parents was the day that he finally heard the boy speak.

Elias had run his fingers over the wooden case and said, *"Do you want me to play for you?"*

Speechless, Zhao Jiangsu had nodded.

The music that Elias played that day stunned him. The boy was a maestro. Even with his untrained ear, he could see that Elias was a prodigy, someone who should raise to the height of fame with the kind of talent he had. After Elias had played a tune on his violin that Zhao Jiangsu did not recognise but would not forget for the rest of his life, the two sat back in their seats and smiled at each other.

"I am Elias," the young boy said politely, extending his hand toward the older man.

Zhao Jiangsu smiled his characteristic smile that turned his eyes into half-moons. This was the first time in days and days that he'd felt genuine happiness. He caught the boy's hand and waved it like he would any adult's. *"I am Zhao Jiangsu. You can call me Jiangsu tài."*

Elias nodded and said, *"Do you know how to play the violin?"*

Zhao Jiangsu shook his head and answered, *"I'm sorry I don't. I am not good at playing music. I can only listen to it. But I have a daughter. Her name is Fei. She likes playing the piano sometimes."*

"Oh she does?" Elias asked with wide eyes. *"Then where is she? Maybe we can find a piano for her to play here!"*

Zhao Jiangsu saw the first sign of excitement in the little boy's eyes. This was an indication that the boy was slowly but surely coming back to life. The older man was glad that the boy was going to be okay. He said, *"She isn't here. But she lives with her mother in Yancheng. In a few days, I am going to Yancheng to be with them."*

When the young boy looked at him with wide eyes that had a look of accusation in them, he smiled and added, *"Would you come with me?"*

Elias's face immediately brightened. He had felt abandoned in those few moments before Zhao Jiangsu had extended the offer to him. He gave a small smile and nodded, *"Yes, please. Thank you."*

Zhao Jiangsu laughed at the child's politeness and sweetness. Then he got up from his chair and headed out, already making plans to make his way out of Nanking with his as well as Elias's limbs and life intact.

***

Zhao Jiangsu sighed as he finished recounting his time at the safety zone. His throat was dry because he had talked much more than he was accustomed to. He looked at Elias who was watching him with a grateful smile on his face.

"And so you saved me," Elias spoke, the smile still lingering on his face.

The old man touched Elias's shoulder and answered solemnly, *"No, Elias, you saved me."*

As Elias drove his car to his apartment that night, the two men had lapsed into an easy silence. It was comfortable to not speak. Each felt so relaxed in the other's company that they didn't always need words to fill up the quiet. Elias thought about the journey to Yancheng. It was as if a new world had opened up before him.

There was bad there but there was also good. As he reminisced about his past, he finally came to the conclusion that Zhao Jiangsu had wanted him to accept for very long: the time had again come – the time for him to change his life.

Chapter 12
Letting Go

"I think we should get back home now," Elias said as he turned to face the road again. Sometime during their discussion, it had started and then stopped raining. Now, the skies looked clear and cloudless. Though dusk was approaching, Elias felt it was the time of dawn which brings the hope of a new start.

Zhao Jiangsu cleared his throat. Then he yawned before covering his mouth like a child. *"Yes. Fei and Lois are still at the apartment. Fei can talk when she wants to talk to people. So the two girls might have got along well with each other."*

"I doubt that," Elias mumbled and put the car in ignition. He knew Fei to be a friendly person from the days that he had spent in his childhood with her. And even now during the visits with Elias, she had been very gracious and sociable. He couldn't say the same about Lois though. She was only sociable when she had something to gain from the other person.

She would have sized Fei up and decided this Chinese woman would not help her cause of social climbing. Even so, he expected Lois to have kept a pretence of civility. If anything, impressions were the most important thing for Lois, Elias thought, and she might have worked to keep up her own impression.

"It seems like several days have passed, not just a few hours," Elias commented after about fifteen minutes of quietly driving on the streets that were almost empty. He thought about this trip that had revealed more about his life and himself to Elias than he could ever have predicted. It felt like an emotional journey to him. He wasn't the same person at the end of it that he was at the start. It was, Elias decided, a journey of self-revelation.

In his peripheral vision, he saw Zhao Jiangsu nod. The old man said, *"That's how it is when you talk of the past. Your hours turn into days, into weeks, into entire lives…"*

Elias understood what he was saying. He had spent the last several hours going over the events of his early life – the most important time of his entire existence. It wasn't exactly possible to condense all that had happened into those few hours but talking about it made him feel as if he had travelled a long distance in a matter of minutes. He felt emotionally drained and physically exhausted. He wanted to bury himself under covers and sleep his exhaustion away.

There was so much for him to do now – so much to change, work on, and make peace with. *'Time,'* he wondered, *'is the only thing. All that I learned today opened the old wounds. But then, all the things Jiangsu tài told me sutured the wounds again. Now I can let myself heal, finally.'*

He pulled into the parking area of his apartment building. Manoeuvring the car into the parking spot, Elias prayed for Lois to have left already. He really did not want to deal with her drama at present. Knowing Lois, there was no guarantee she wouldn't throw a fit at how many hours Elias had been away, leaving her stranded with his Chinese friend.

He helped Jiangsu tài out of the car and entered the elevator. He got off on the right floor and made his way to the door, with Zhao Jiangsu in tow. Ringing the doorbell, he waited for Lois to answer. But when the door opened in a few moments, he found Fei standing there alone. Elias smiled at her and stood to the side to let Zhao Jiangsu pass first. Then he motioned Fei to enter and closed the door behind him.

"You two were away longer than I thought you would be," Fei said, taking a seat on the sofa beside her father.

"Yes, we were catching up with each other," Zhao Jiangsu said.

Elias smiled and said, *"I hope you weren't worried. I took good care of your father."*

"Oh, I have no doubt that you did," Fei answered.

"Yes, yes. He is like my son, he took better care of me than even you," Zhao Jiangsu said with mock seriousness. Fei pretended to look offended, making Elias laugh.

"That's not true. He told me how much care you take of his medicines. He also said how you monitor what he should eat and shouldn't eat. I can't even come close to being so devoted," Elias said.

"Oh, so he was complaining about me?" Fei grumbled, getting a laugh out of Elias who shook his head in the negative, even though what Fei had said wasn't that far from the truth.

Elias looked around the apartment but found no sign of Lois. He cleared his throat and asked, *"Where is Lois? Did she leave already?"*

"*Yes, she left quite a long while ago, actually. She barely stayed an hour after you were gone,*" Fei said, picking up the magazine on the coffee table. She began to skim through the magazine, which was full of coloured pictures of historical buildings in the city of New York. There were also detailed descriptions of when and why those buildings were constructed along with the pictures. Fei seemed engrossed; it seemed that she liked the subject of History.

"*Oh,*" Elias said. Then he dropped the subject. He didn't want to ask Fei if Lois had behaved politely with her or if she had thrown a fit.

After a while, Fei began talking on her own. She spoke in English, indicating she didn't want her father to understand what she was saying, "*I don't know if it is my place to say it Elias, but your girlfriend...she did not have good things to say about you.*"

Elias took a breath to prepare himself for the worst. It had not occurred to him that Lois might talk about him behind his back to his own guest. He affected nonchalance as he asked, "*Oh, is that so? What did she say?*"

"Well, among other things," Fei started, fidgeting in her place, looking very uncomfortable with the situation she had been put in, *"She said you were a drunkard...and a drug abuser. 'Druggie' was the term she used, I believe."*

Elias looked at Fei who had turned red from embarrassment. She clearly hadn't wanted to repeat the information but for some reason, she had. He gave a self-deprecating smile before admitting, *"And what if I told you all that is true?"* Elias felt insulted but he didn't also didn't want to hide from the truth though Lois had put it in very ugly and harsh words.

Maintaining her poise, Fei said, *"That, I believe, is none of my business. My point here isn't to learn of all your flaws, or to determine what might be wrong in your relationship with your girlfriend. It is only when she said those things I felt really awkward."*

"You felt awkward?" Elias interjected. He wasn't surprised, though. He had not expected Fei to be the kind of person who would enjoy gossip.

"Yes, of course. These things aren't for me to know," Fei asserted, sitting straight up to make her point.

Elias replied generously, *"You can know them, Fei. I already talked to Jiangsu tài about it. He knows the truth."*

"That's not the point. You told my father but that's between you and him. Anyway, I don't want to turn you against your girlfriend. I only hope you two will resolve whatever is wrong so that you two can keep your private life private."

Elias nodded, understanding Fei's point. Lois's unjustified blabbering had undoubtedly made Fei feel as if she were caught in the crossfire between two opposing armies. Lois was never one to know what to say to someone and what not. Fei just didn't want to be part of their private disputes – and that's what she was telling Elias who knew she was right in her place.

Elias glanced at Zhao Jiangsu. The old man looked piercingly at Elias, and Elias saw that he had understood all that had been said between Fei and Elias thought they had been talking in a language he didn't know. Maybe that was the insight one gained with old age and experience, Elias decided, as he said to his guests, *"I hope you will stay for drinks?"*

"No, thank you," Fei said.

At the same time as Fei, Zhao Jiangsu said, *"Yes, Baijiu for me."*

Elias laughed as Fei looked exasperatedly at her father who pointedly ignored her. Elias said, *"I am sorry I don't have Baijiu, Jiangsu tài. But I have white wine, I think you will like it."*

The old man nodded eagerly as Fei tried in vain to hide the cross expressions on her face. She stood up from the sofa and said, *"I'll say goodbye now. I hope Father will join me downstairs in five minutes. The car is waiting for us."*

"Yes, I will take five minutes only," Zhao Jiangsu said magnanimously to his daughter. Fei rolled her eyes and said bye to Elias before leaving the apartment.

Elias opened the vintage bottle of white wine that he had been saving for quite some time. Then he poured it into one glass and handed it to Zhao Jiangsu who looked at him knowingly, *"Only one glass?"*

"Yes," Elias said with a small smile. *"I might as well start changing things from today rather than wait for tomorrow."*

"That's my boy," Zhao Jiangsu said with a twinkle of pride in his eyes. *"Your parents will be proud of you."*

"I hope so," Elias said. The thought of putting his life back in order was daunting but he was determined to make a change now.

"This is the time that I should tell you…" Zhao Jiangsu said hesitantly.

"Tell me what?" Elias asked, his interest piqued by the old man's cautious approach.

"There is an old tradition in China, the country of your birth, of ancestor veneration. You know we hold family close to our hearts, even when they have crossed over from this world to the next."

"Yes, I do know," Elias nodded. *"There were many neighbours during my childhood who had altars in their homes dedicated to their dead ancestors. I remember asking my mother about it and her explaining it to me."*

"So what do you think of it?"

"I think it's a beautiful way to keep all those that are gone in your thoughts.'

"Yes, Elias. It's a way also to thank them. We carry a spiritual debt to our ancestors and it is our duty to pay back to them. Did you ever think about it in relation to your parents?"

Elias answered, "No, I didn't think of doing that. I was too busy running away from the memories of my past that I hardly ever mourned my parents properly, Jiangsu tài.'

The old man nodded sympathetically then added, "Yes, I understand that. I want to tell you that I did that for you. I got your parents' names inscribed on a tablet which I keep next to the names of my own ancestors in the alcove in my home."

Elias was struck silent by this information. He had not expected anybody to honour his parents like this. He gulped to swallow the lump that rose in his throat. When he spoke his voice was hoarse with emotion, "Thank you, Jiangsu tài. I don't know what to say."

"You don't need to say anything. You only need to honour your parents in your own way. You know what that is, don't you?"

Elias shook his head like a child.

Zhao Jiangsu smiled and said, *"You just have to repay them by living a good and happy life. So cut out all the bad things – alcohol, drugs, or wrong relationships. Do things that bring you peace and happiness and that don't harm you in any way. I can't imagine any other thing that would make your parents happy."*

Elias didn't say anything but only nodded. He listened as Zhao Jiangsu told him about the teacups he had put around the name tablets, and the flowers he offered there every Sunday. He also listened about how Zhao Jiangsu lit incense around the private shrine on the Chinese New Year, as a way to celebrate the life of the deceased.

After explaining to Elias how these acts of veneration would bring peace to the soul of the dead, Zhao Jiangsu relaxed back in his chair and sipped quietly at his wine. He seemed in no hurry to leave, and Elias smiled at the indifference with which he let his daughter Fei wait for him. There seemed to be a lot of love but also a kind of rivalry between father and daughter – and this made Elias decide that they behaved less like parent and child and more like siblings who fought than made up just as easily. Finally, the old man finished his drink and then stood up to leave.

On his way out of the door, he slapped Elias on the back for his good decision to change his life. Elias smiled and escorted him downstairs, despite his protestations that he wasn't that old and could take the elevator on his own. Elias reminded him how in China it wouldn't be considered good manners to let your guests leave without showing them proper respect.

He helped Zhao Jiangsu into the car, thanked both him and Fei and then waved them bye. Then he went back to his apartment and closed the door with a decisive thud. This sound, he felt, heralded a new beginning for him.

***

The next morning, Elias ate his breakfast in welcome solitude. He watched the bare apartment, and noticed that it was distinctly devoid of any stamp of his personality. He felt as if he were looking at everything for the first time.

Indulging in his vices for so long had numbed him to the extent that he barely even took note of his surroundings. In running away from his past, he had unknowingly been running away from himself. Overnight, he had decided to seek help for his addictions.

He had a new resolve to live a clean life – one where no such dependences would take him away from his true purpose. He saw how, all along, it was music that had saved him, and not alcohol or drugs. Those had been mere distractions which kept him tethered to the wrong things and wrong places. He had told Zhao Jiangsu the same yesterday – how music had become his salvation. From the time that his parents had died, he had relied on his violin to make it through life.

He walked to the built-in bar, his mind once more lost in the recollection of his past. He picked up the bottles one by one automatically, as though compelled by some spell. He walked to the sink in the kitchen and began to empty the bottles one by one. He didn't care how much money he had spent on purchasing these drinks. He only wanted to be rid of the demon that had had hold of him for too many years to count.

As he performed this cleansing ritual of sorts, his mind was invaded by those long-buried notes of music. An image from the past rose up in his mind, that of himself playing the violin for his parents. Both his mother and father often requested him to play this or that song for him. Countless times, he had played them a sweet, sad melody on his violin – his father loved that one tune the best. Elias thought about the name of it but could not recall it. He only remembered the notes that spilt longing and sadness into the room and filled it up like air. He could still see his father, eyes closed and swaying to the music. He could see his mother's gaze fixed on the wall and a small smile playing around her lips, as she became lost in the tune and thought of times past.

He had overheard his mother say that the particular melody always reminded her of the time of her childhood in Russia. And now, the tune reminded Elias of his childhood in China. Even today, the notes of the song that he used to play for his parents haunted him. That was one song that he had not been able to play publicly in America.

It was too private. But now, as he was coming to terms with his old grief, he wanted to play the tune. It wouldn't be for himself but for his dead parents. After Elias was done draining all the alcohol out of his life, he threw away the one small pack of marijuana that he had in the apartment. Just a week ago, he had been planning to get more from the dealer who was a telephone call away from him. But he knew he wouldn't do that anymore.

He felt strangely light, as though a big invisible boulder had been removed from his shoulders. Optimistic about his progress so far, he decided to make the third and the final decision of his life for today.

He called Lois.

"Well, well, well. Look who's called," Lois greeted him with as much sarcasm as she could muster. Elias admitted he had never quite heard Lois being so directly bitter and angry.

'So this means I seriously offended her yesterday,' Elias thought before he said, *"What's wrong with you, Lois?"*

"You left me with your guest last afternoon. Do you expect me to play host for you?"

"What's wrong with that? Aren't you my girlfriend?"

"Am I your girlfriend? You don't love me, Elias. Let's not pretend otherwise. So no, I will not play host for you when you don't even give me any of the privileges that a girlfriend deserves."

Elias took the receiver away from his ear and stared at it in disbelief. Then he put it back to his ear and said, *"I'm sorry but what privileges are those?"*

Lois remained sullenly silent. He knew from experience that Lois preferred to use the silent treatment as one of her strategies to have the upper hand in any situation.

"What did you say to Fei about me?" Elias asked, though he did not really care to know her side of the story.

"Oh so that high and mighty miss told on me, did she?"

"If that's what you want to think. But did you or didn't you say those things to her?"

"I did. What's wrong with that? Aren't they true?"

"Yes, they are true. You know Lois, we have wasted enough of each other's time. I believe you deserve someone who'd be more accommodating toward your wishes than I am. And I certainly can do without you."

"What are you saying?"

"I am saying I am calling this sham of a relationship off. We need to be as far away from each other as we can, instead of being together."

From her offended silence, Elias could tell Lois was taken aback. If he knew her – and he did – she'd have wanted to be the one to end things rather than hearing it from him. Elias did a small inner dance of victory at beating her to it. From her recent behaviour, he had got the idea that she would take the step soon anyway. So this decision, he knew, would not hurt anything but Lois's pride. The way Elias saw it, he was doing both himself and her a favour. He also knew Lois must have some alternate for him available already or she wouldn't have shown her resentment toward him so openly. She was, Elias still admitted, the kind of a woman who could wrap any man around her fingers. Elias had failed her in that regard – and Lois had never quite forgiven him for falling out of infatuation with her so fast.

"Fine, Elias. You're a complete jerk and I hope you know that!" Lois said before slamming the phone down on him.

Elias shrugged and put the receiver back with deliberate carefulness. He felt as if the last load had been lifted off him.

He got up from the sofa and walked to the tall windows that he always kept curtained. He liked the dark. For years, he had kept away from light as much as he could. So all the rooms in his apartment had thick drapes that always kept sunlight out. The atmosphere of gloom was preserved in this way. He liked it because that's how he was able to match his outer surroundings with his inner state. But now, he put both his hands on the curtains and pulled them open. Bright sunlight spilt into the room, and got into Elias's eyes. It wasn't uninvited. Elias squinted from the feeling of discomfort. However, after standing resolutely in the sun for a few minutes, his eyes became acquainted with the brilliance of the day.

He no longer felt pain at being exposed to light. He felt clearheaded as though he, too, were flooded with a brightness that he had never experienced before. The shadows lifted and for the first time in a long time, he saw everything illuminated.

Chapter 13
Long Way Around

"But how did you two escape Nanking?" Fei asked, stirring her lemonade with the straw.

Elias and Zhao Jiangsu looked at each other. The three of them were at a local Italian restaurant. The weather was good, so they'd decided to have an alfresco lunch. Before this, Elias had accompanied both his Chinese guests to the Lincoln Memorial and the National Gallery of Art. Fei had loved the gallery and was especially fascinated by the Sculpture Garden.

Elias said, *"Well, you know…"*

Fei leaned forward in her chair and eagerly said, *"No, that's it, I don't know! Father never told me the story of the escape. I imagine it was very adventurous."*

Zhao Jiangsu snorted. *"Adventurous. She calls it adventurous,"* he remarked looking at Elias.

"Please quit talking about me as if I'm not here," Fei said stiffly, crossing her arms over her chest.

Zhao Jiangsu laughed, pleased to have got to his daughter who usually remained calm and unperturbed as a smooth lake.

"I'm sorry, Fei," Elias said, shaking his head at the old man's ongoing tussle with his daughter. *"Adventurous isn't quite the word I'd use to describe the journey, though."*

"It was dangerous! At every turn, danger lurked! Even our own shadows looked like enemies! To this day, I do not know how we made it!" Zhao Jiangsu said, banging his fist on the table.

Elias rolled his eyes at Fei, making sure Zhao Jiangsu didn't see. Though the journey was full of peril, it was nowhere near as dramatic as the old man had made it out to be. For the most part, they moved so fast from one place to another that even the dangers didn't have enough time to register on them. It was only in the aftermath of the risky flight, when they were in a relatively safe place, that Elias was hit by the enormity of what he had survived.

"It was a difficult journey," Elias said with much more modesty than Zhao Jiangsu.

"I remember it was the end of May. The weather was hot, especially so during the day," Zhao Jiangsu added.

"It was the Year of the Tiger," Elias smiled, remembering the small detail that he had forgotten over the years.

"That it was," Zhao Jiangsu nodded. *"I was scared, more for Elias than myself. I had promised his mother I'd look after him."*

Elias smiled. *"I remember we left the hospital grounds in bright daylight. Dressed in rags, like beggars who had nothing anybody would want to steal. Jiangsu tài had a walking stick."*

"You escaped in the day? Why not at night? Wouldn't that have been safer?" Fei enquired.

"It wasn't. The city gates were opened during the day. It was only opened so that produce from farmers in the countryside could be brought in this city," Zhao Jiangsu said.

Fei looked at Elias and then at her father before she settled in her chair. *"Start from the beginning,"* she said.

"Well, it was a normal day at the hospital..." Elias started.

***

On this regular day at the hospital, Elias was sitting in his room on the narrow bed. He was still weak but could walk around now. The doctors were satisfied with the progress and didn't check up on him as frequently as they did before.

Elias looked up as Zhao Jiangsu entered the room quickly. His eyes darted here and there as if to make sure there was no one in the room except for Elias. He then hurried over to the bedside and caught Elias's hand. *"How do you feel today, wŏ de háizi?"*

Elias noticed something irregular about the old man's behaviour. He was jumpy today, and nervous, as though he were standing on the brink of an edge. He politely said, *"I am well, Jiangsu tài. And how are you?"*

"I am well, yes. I came here to tell you that we leave today, my child."

"Leave?" Elias repeated.

"Yes, yes. Do you remember when I told you I am going where my family is to Yancheng?"

Elias nodded. Zhao Jiangsu grabbed his arm, *"So we leave today, my child. In fact, we leave in an hour. The time is right. I'll ask you to do exactly as I say. You will listen to me, won't you?"*

Again, Elias nodded. He trusted Jiangsu tài almost as much as he trusted his own father. So he didn't question him, though he did feel a little scared. The hospital seemed like a safe place for him, and he had got used to the routine there. He'd just settled in, and he was being asked to move again. As Zhao Jiangsu left Elias sighed. Then he looked around the small room and said goodbye to the now-familiar bed, walls, windows, and one chair. He already knew he'd never be back here again.

***

Clutching Elias's hand in a too-tight grip, Zhao Jiangsu walked out the doors of the hospital. Elias looked up at the man who had exchanged his old clothes for a tattered tunic. Zhao Jiangsu looked nothing like a soldier after he had transformed into a beggar's getup. He was also very thin, so much so that his cheekbones jutted out sharply from his face, and that gave him an appropriately haggard look. He had made Elias change into very old, dirty clothes too – which Elias had no idea where he had obtained from. Then, to Elias's surprise, he'd smeared both their faces with dirt. He hadn't stopped there but had smeared Elias's reddish hair with ash and dirt. He finished his own look by carrying a crude walking stick made out of a thick branch of a tree.

By the time he was finished, both of them had looked like a very sorry, down-on-their-luck, pair. Zhao Jiangsu walked so fast that Elias had difficulty keeping pace with him. He felt that instead of walking himself he was more being dragged along the muddy path. He turned his neck from time to time to look at the bright red flag of the Red Cross that flew from the top of the hospital building until it completely vanished from his sight.

His legs hurt from all the walking and sweat ran down his face but he didn't say a word. Zhao Jiangsu had told him to remain quiet until he told Elias it was safe to talk. Huffing by now, Zhao Jiangsu ignored the cramp in his left leg and continued to march ahead. Several more people were going the same way, and he knew they were all escaping under the same disguise as he was. He was headed toward the southwestern gate of the city where he knew guards stood at attention. They were after smugglers, though, and Zhao Jiangsu had nothing but the clothes on his back and Elias's wooden violin case which he'd put inside a sack of rotting vegetables that he carried over one shoulder. He had full hopes the guards would let them pass, taking them to be poor dirt farmers.

Elias and the older man reached the gate and passed without incident. Zhao Jiangsu did not believe his good luck! He didn't look up yet for he knew they were still in the line of sight of the guards and who knew when they might change their minds? He kept his head down and kept walking in a straight line. He had reached a considerable distance from the gates when behind him he heard a loud scream of agony.

Without looking, he knew one of the escapees had been caught by the guard. Zhao Jiangsu grabbed Elias's hand more tightly and took off. He ran, and he ran without knowing if they were being followed. He walked into the forest that lined the road and kept walking deeper into it. It was perhaps a half an hour later that he looked around. When he saw they were alone in the forest, he stopped. He left

Elias's hand and collapsed on the muddy ground. Elias sat down beside him and looked at his sweaty face worriedly. He still didn't say a word.

"It's all right, Elias, you can talk now," Zhao Jiangsu said as he tried to draw deep breaths.

"Where…where are we?"

"We are on our way to Yancheng," Zhao Jiangsu replied. That's all he knew at this time. He had mapped his way to the city, but he didn't know precisely where they were at the moment. He was waiting for nightfall when he and Elias could leave the forest and walk to the main path which would lead away from Nanking.

The next few days passed in a blur. The only thing Elias could recall from those endless afternoons and nights was walking. He walked, and he walked, and he walked until his feet were scraped raw. On his way, he saw many people like himself and Zhao Jiangsu. Each looked as hungry and helpless as Elias felt. They barely rested, and they barely ate. Elias became habitual of the clawing feeling of hunger in the pit of his stomach. On some days if he was lucky he got to eat a bowl of fermented rice twice. On most days, the meals were restricted to one bowl per day. For their food, they depended wholly on the kindness of strangers who, for the most part, were as impoverished and starving as themselves. It was two weeks after they had left the city of Nanking that Elias came across the biggest flood he'd ever seen. It was as if the river had opened up its giant mouth and swallowed up everything in its path; and now, there was only water as far as the eye could see.

There used to be a thin river here, Zhao Jiangsu told him, but now it had swelled. This was a city called Yangzhou, and it was located near the northern bank of the River Yangtze. The city, Zhao Jiangsu informed Elias, was lined with canals and small lakes. It was also occupied by the Japanese, so they kept out of it.

It was one morning, as they were walking in the northeast direction, that Elias heard loud popping sounds, as though hundreds of big bubbles were being burst one by one. This was followed by the sound of gushing water – unstoppable, endless, and angry. Elias felt as if ten thousand galloping horses were headed their way, ready to trample them down. The noise was deafening, and the fear in Elias's heart very real. Hairs on the back of his arm stood up as he waited for the horses to reach them. It was only later that he learned the popping bubbles were the dykes on River Yangtze being breached, and the sound of the horses' hooves beating against the ground was the flood that changed the course of China's history. Elias climbed atop a small hill and saw that every land area in the far distance was inundated.

He told Zhao Jiangsu that he could see people floating upon the surface of the water, but the older man told him it was only his imagination. *"Those aren't people,"* Zhao Jiangsu said, *"but debris. You know, from houses and such that were destroyed by the flood."* Elias nodded as if he understood every word even though he didn't. He still thought there were people – and dead ones with their bloated bodies – drifting on the floodwater because they could no longer swim. He didn't insist his point, however, and pretended that he accepted what Zhao Jiangsu had told him.

"When will we get to Yancheng?" he asked Zhao Jiangsu, perhaps for the hundredth time. Elias had never thought the journey would take this long. He was getting more impatient by the day. He just didn't want to keep walking anymore.

"We are almost there, my child," Zhao Jiangsu said. He knew the trip would take a few more days still, but he knew

Elias was at the end of his tether. Their pace had been slowed considerably by first the threat of the Japanese and then by the flood. He had heard from farmers he had met along the way that the dykes on the Yangtze River had been breached. He had listened in disbelief when the old farmer had told him it was no one else but the Chinese nationalists that had caused the flood.

"But didn't they think of how many would die?" Zhao Jiangsu said, enraged.

The old farmer sighed. *"What has this nation been doing for years but bear the dead? They must have thought those who would die because of the floods are no different than who are already killed."*

Try as he did, Zhao Jiangsu could not understand the rationale behind the decision. He thought of how many areas would be underwater, how many homes and living sources would be destroyed, and how many people would drown or die of water-borne diseases. It was too much – too high a cost for what was not even a victory over the Japanese but only another stalling measure. There wasn't anything that he could do about it, however, so he kept walking to Yancheng.

The closer he got to his family, the more he wanted to live. He just couldn't wait to see his daughter and his wife again. Zhao Jiangsu and Elias entered the city of Yancheng a little after midnight. The streets were dark and deserted, but Zhao Jiangsu made his way to his old home relying on his memory. He told Elias he could walk to his home in his sleep – that's how well he knew it. Elias wondered what his home was and if he, too, could walk there in his sleep but he came up with no good answer.

In the dim moonlight that spilt on the narrow street, Elias saw they had stopped before the wooden door of a small house. Zhao Jiangsu took a deep breath and rapped on the wood twice in quick succession. Then he stepped away from the door and rested against the main walls of the house, as though hiding from view. Elias did the same.

The door opened a crack, and a small voice said, *"Who is this?"*

Beside him, Elias felt the older man shudder. Zhao Jiangsu then stepped away from the shadows and in front of the barely-open door. Next, Elias heard a yelp before the door was opened wide and Zhao Jiangsu was wrapped in the arms of a muscular woman.

As the older man was still holding Elias's arm, he got pulled inside at the same time. The door was shut, but Zhao Jiangsu was still being smothered by this woman who just would not let him go. Furthermore, the weeping woman also made no sense to Elias though she kept up a constant commentary. She was blubbering, and Zhao Jiangsu was trying to quiet her down.

Elias pulled so he could tug his hand away from Zhao Jiangsu – he really did not want to be the next one to be smothered so by the woman – but he found he didn't have to. Zhao Jiangsu let him go easily and proceeded to wrap his arm, now that it was free of Elias, around the woman, soothing her like he would a crying child.

Elias looked around the small room which was poorly lit by a single lamp. He couldn't make much out except for the silhouette of a few pieces of furniture. He turned around and was almost scared out of his life when he saw two penetrating eyes looking right at him. He could make nothing of the face as of yet but could see the eyes that looked searchingly at him.

It was a girl. Elias realized it as soon as she said, *"Who are you?"*

Of course! Elias thought. This must be Zhao Jiangsu's daughter!

Elias bowed as his parents had taught him before he said, *"I am Elias. Are you Fei?"*

The girl nodded several times. Then she asked, *"But how do you know?"*

Elias pointed at Zhao Jiangsu who was now finally out of the woman's arms and was busy telling her how he'd come to be here at this time of the night. *"Jiangsu tài told me."*

"How do you know him?" the curious girl with the endless questions asked him next.

Elias didn't know what to say, so he looked at the older man for help. Zhao Jiangsu, luckily, came to his rescue. He opened his arms to his daughter and said, *"Won't you say hello and welcome home to your father, Fei?"*

Fei leapt into her father's arms. Then she kissed both his cheeks and politely asked him how he was. Zhao Jiangsu ran his hand over her hair and said she looked taller than he had left her. Then he asked her how she was and Fei launched into a whole tale about all that had happened in her father's absence.

From the corner of his eyes, Elias saw that the fat woman was looking at her husband and daughter lovingly. Elias suddenly felt out of place, as though he did not belong here. Tears pricked his eyes as he thought of his own mother and father. He turned away toward the door. Just then, Zhao Jiangsu reached out and caught Elias's arm, forcing Elias to turn to him.

"And this!" Zhao Jiangsu proudly announced, as though Elias were a particularly bright jewel in an emperor's crown, *"this is Elias. Say hello to him, Fei."*

"Hello, Elias," Fei said, bowing to him.

Zhao Jiangsu turned to his wife and said, *"Do you have anything to eat?"*

The woman nodded and went into a small room to the side which obviously served as the kitchen. Zhao Jiangsu followed the woman. From where Elias was, he could hear the two of them talking, but he could not make out the words.

He wondered if Zhao Jiangsu was telling his wife about him and if she would tell him to throw the kid out. He wondered what would happen if Zhao Jiangsu actually did that. His thoughts were interrupted by Fei who poked his arm with her finger. *"Who are you?"* she said.

"I am...Elias," he repeated, wondering if the girl were so forgetful that she'd forgotten his name though he'd told her only a few minutes ago.

"I know, but none of my friends has such a name!" she said.

Elias, like the first time, went quite speechless. He again had nothing to say to the girl who was as bright as she was pretty.

"So, what do you like to play?" she asked next, before telling him she liked hopscotch.

"I like playing my violin!" Elias responded, happy to have an answer at last.

"Violin?" the girl repeated, as though it were a foreign word to her.

Elias nodded and said, *"I can show it to you if you like."*

"Yes, please," she answered solemnly.

Elias reached into the dirty sack that he and Zhao Jiangsu had left the hospital with. He saw the girl wrinkle her nose at the gross smell that emerged out of the bag and suppressed a smile. Proudly, he withdrew the wooden case out of the sack and sat down on the floor with it on his lap. Fei watched with keen eyes as Elias opened the lid of the case and removed a shiny musical instrument from it.

"Do you want me to play it for you?" Elias whispered to Fie.

"*Yes!*" Fei said.

Elias rested the violin against his chin although it was too big for him and put his bow against the strings. He closed his eyes and began to play. He had only played a few notes when he felt someone taking the violin away from him. He opened his eyes and saw it was Zhao Jiangsu.

He smiled apologetically and said, *"I am sorry, Elias. But don't play the violin in here right now. It's night, and the mystic travels far and wide. People will suspect. Come morning, they will start looking."*

Elias nodded although he felt heartbroken that Zhao Jiangsu had stopped him from playing the violin. The older man rested his hand on Elias's head for a few seconds and said, *"You can play it in the morning, I promise."*

Fei, however, was already impressed by Elias's skill. She exclaimed, *"Can you teach me? I want to learn! Elias, tomorrow I'll take you to meet my friends, and you can play your violin in front of them, and they will see how amazing it is, too!"*

Zhao Jiangsu turned toward his wife and said, *"As I just told you, we need to leave before more days pass. I have already decided on Hong Kong. That's the safest spot in the country."*

"And how will we go there?" Fei's mother, whose name was Ling, asked.

"By junk," Zhao Jiangsu said. *"It will leave from the port of Yancheng in a week. Before that, you and Fei – and you, too, Elias – you all have to keep quiet about the plan. I don't want people to know where you are going and when. We will leave at night so that we are undetected."*

Ling nodded while Fei stared at her father. It was slowly dawning on her that her father had said they would leave their home. That would mean leaving her friends, and her games, and her neighbour's cat who was more hers than theirs. Her smile changed into a frown, and in a few moments, she began to cry.

"Shhh...my child," Zhao Jiangsu said, leaning down, so he was at Fei's height before he began to dry her tears off with his hands. *"It's going be fine, my daughter. Your father is here with you."* Fei wrapped her arms around her father's neck as she sobbed, sad beyond anything she had ever been.

Ling, who was double the size of her husband, turned toward Elias. For the first time, she smiled at him and said, *"Hello, Elias. Welcome to our home. Are you hungry?"*

Elias looked at her with surprise in his eyes. He had for some reason expected her to be mad at her husband for bringing him to her home without her permission. But she was very welcoming and motherly. Elias nodded.

In a few minutes, Ling brought out a bowl of boiled rice and vegetable soup. It wasn't a lot, but it was fresh, and it smelled delicious. Elias scooped up the hot rice in his hands and began to eat. So did Zhao Jiangsu. They both were famished, and it showed. Elias ate so quickly that he almost choked on his food. Fei quickly got him water. He gulped it down and listened as Fei instructed like an old grandmother, *"You shouldn't eat so fast, Elias. It gets stuck in your throat."* Elias nodded and then he really did slow down. He began to savour every bite and felt waves of gratitude rise in his heart. He'd appreciated food before but never like this. He had gone on so long without eating properly that a meal, which was meagre by any standards, looked like the biggest luxury to him.

As they finished up eating, Fei and Ling brought out some covers and arranged them on the ground. No sooner was Elias done with the dinner that he crawled underneath into the first soft bedding he'd had in a while and went to sleep. He slept as peacefully as though he were back in his parents' house.

***

"And the next morning I woke up to the sound of Fei yelling," Elias said.

"I did not yell!" Fei protested, sitting up in her chair. Elias stifled his laughter at Fei's indignant reaction. She stuck her nose in the air and said, *"For your information, it was a very big bug, and it was right on top of your head!"*

"Yes, and it was about to devour you whole, Elias!" Zhao Jiangsu said dramatically.

"Stop it, you two! I just got worried. Elias was a guest. If he'd been harmed in our house the very first day, what would he think about us?" she explained.

"I am still very grateful to you for saving me," Elias smiled.

"And he's also very grateful for the red welt that you left when you swatted the fly with your fan on his face!" Zhao Jiangsu interjected cheerfully.

As Fei looked at him with wounded eyes, Elias laughed. The father and daughter duo really took their animosity too far. They fought like little kids, and Elias had to play the mediator – not that he didn't enjoy the role, but sometimes it got trickier when one or the other wanted him to take sides.

"How did you like lunch?" Elias asked Fei, changing the topic of conversation.

"It was very delicious, thank you very much! The best I've had in a while, let me add," Fei smiled graciously.

Elias wanted to add that no food could ever in his mind compare to that bowl of rice that Fei's dear mother had prepared for him that night. However, he did not mention it. They had talked about the ordeal of getting out of Nanking and into Yancheng over their lunch. Elias had become so engrossed in the old tale that he'd barely tasted his food. He paid the bill, insisting when his guests protested at his generosity and steered them into his car to drive them to their hotel.

As he heard Fei and Zhao Jiangsu start to bicker again, he smiled to himself. Looking at them, he wondered, *'Where and who would I be if not for these two people, their kind family?'*

'Not here, and not me,' he decided and began to drive on the immaculate streets of DC.

Chapter 14
The First Song

"This coffee is really good," Fei said, sipping on her Americano.

"I knew you would like it," Elias said, tapping the table with his fingers in time to the tune that had come into his head just now as he was looking at Fei. They had met up for morning coffee, as they had been doing for some days now. They also met for lunch or dinner on most days. Fei seemed to enjoy his company as much as he enjoyed hers. She looked particularly beautiful today to Elias, dressed in an apricot coat which brought out the pink in her cheeks. She looked fresh and happy, and Elias felt lighter just looking at her.

"Father told me you broke up with Lois?" Fei said, looking at him with concern on her face.

Elias waved his hand in the air as if to ward off a fly. *"That's done and dusted with,"* he said. *"That relationship ended a long time ago."*

"But are you all right, Elias?" Fei said, leaning toward him and putting her hand on his arm to comfort him.

Elias peeked at her hand on his arm and felt his heart skip a beat. For some time now, he had been feeling this way about Fei. He liked being with her, and he liked her concern for him. He liked her when every morning she asked him if he'd slept well, and if he'd had breakfast. In many ways she was the same as she was all those years ago when Elias had stayed with her family. Back then, she had taken him under her wing when they were in Yancheng; she had continued to worry over him in Hong Kong. Elias had had a case of puppy love for her and was heartbroken when he'd come to America, leaving her behind. And now, she was back in his life like she'd never left.

Only a few days ago, Elias had realised that he had fallen in love with Fei. He knew he loved her the way he had never loved another woman. Fei, too, had been spending more and more time with him when Zhao Jiangsu was away on official meetings that had started in earnest. Zhao Jiangsu was going to be in America for several more months at least and Fei's plans to stay behind with her father had delighted Elias. He finally had someone to call his own in the form of Jiangsu tài and Fei – a family like he'd never had before in America.

"I am perfectly fine, Fei," Elias said as he smiled and patted her hand. *"You saw me and Lois. There was no love between us. It was not there to begin with. There was just some attraction that faded away a long time ago,"* he explained in detail. *"I feel very free after breaking up with her for good."*

"Then why did you wait so long to do it?" Fei asked, surprised. Elias knew Fei to be a very practical woman. He understood why she didn't comprehend his act of lugging a dead relationship around. She herself tackled even matters of the heart with her mind – which is perhaps why she was single though she'd had no shortage of suitors, as Jiangsu tài had told him one day. He suspected the old man wanted Elias to get together with his daughter. That he had her father's approval gave him some confidence.

Elias sighed. *"I guess it's because...I don't know, I never thought I might fall for someone for real."*

Fei's eyes widened. *"For someone else?"* she repeated. A light blush coloured her face and she looked perturbed.

"Yes, actually," Elias leaned toward her.

His coffee grew cold but he didn't notice. He had a strategy in mind – and he could already see where it might lead him. *"There is a woman."*

"Oh," Fei said stiffly. It was obvious she didn't like the news. She tried to regain her composure as she forced a smile and asked, *"Who is the lucky woman, if I may ask?"*

"But I am not sure if she will also like me," Elias said, neatly sidestepping her question.

"Why won't she!" Fei protested, outraged on his behalf. *"You are a gentle, kind man, Elias. So I am sure she would like you,"* she finished, trying to calm herself down.

Elias bit back his smile at Fei's conflicted reactions. On the one hand, she was clearly upset he had gone and fallen in love with another woman and on the other, she refused to entertain the possibility that that woman wouldn't love him back. He decided to stop teasing her. He whispered, *"So I should tell her?"*

Fei looked away from him and began to search for some non-existent object in her purse. Her hair fell over her face so he could no longer see her face but her voice betrayed the truth that she was disturbed. She said, *"Yes, I think you should tell her."*

"Fei," Elias said, as he caught her arm. She almost jumped up in surprise as Elias's hand slid down to her hand which he held in a gentle grip.

"Ye—yes?" Fei said, faltering at the intense gaze that Elias levelled on her face.

"I am in love with you," Elias confessed. There was no smile on his face anymore; he was too scared of her possible response to feeling the humour in the situation. He watched her face but she appeared to have turned into a stone statue. She was taking an abnormally long time to react, Elias thought, as he waited patiently for her to absorb what he'd just told her.

"Oh," Fei said, finally blinking out of the trance she had fallen into.

"Well...?" Elias said.

"I love you, as well," Fei said in her formal way.

Elias gulped and repeated, *"You do?"*

"Yes," Fei said, fighting back the smile that, at long last, tugged at the corner of her lips.

Elias released the breath he had unconsciously been holding. He smiled fully then, so much that his eyes shone like stars on a cloudless night. He caught both of Fei's hands and said, *"You have just made me so happy, Fei."*

"I know!" Fei laughed, entwining her fingers with his.

"So you will stay with me?" Elias asked, a hint of doubt appearing in his eyes. It wasn't that he didn't trust Fei – it was his fate that was the problem. He had quite simply never been this lucky.

"Yes, I will, Elias. Of course, I will," Fei promised as she laughed.

Elias looked at her as his heart welled up. In his head played the sweetest music – one that spoke of hope, of new beginnings and exquisite longing that ended in harmony. As he kissed Fei, he realised he had rediscovered the music he had been waiting to write for years.

Elias had sheet music spread before him on his small desk. He had begun writing the music the very same that it had surfaced in his mind when he'd admitted his love to Fei that day. A week had passed since then. He had made good progress; even though the work was still unfinished. Now that he was writing music after a break of several long years, Elias felt fully alive. It was true that with Fei and Zhao Jiangsu's arrival in his life he had started to become reacquainted with himself – the person he was, and the musician he was, before he became ensnared by all the addictions that had sucked the life out of him.

He had just finished writing the coda when he heard the doorbell ring. He was not expecting a visitor – very few people dropped by his place, anyway – so he walked to the door a little surprised about who might be there. As soon as he opened the door, his face broke into a fond smile. He reached out and put his arm around the small frame of Zhao Jiangsu.

"What a wonderful surprise, Jiangsu tài!" he said, ushering the old man into his apartment.

"Yes!" Zhao Jiangsu announced. *"I have been very busy with the never-ending meetings. I haven't seen you in ages so I told the chauffeur to drive me here."*

"Good thing you did, Jiangsu tài," Elias said, taking his coat and putting it over the sofa. *"I was missing you, too."*

"Humph!" Zhao Jiangsu said, making a face. *"You only

spend time with Fei now that she is your girlfriend."

Elias almost laughed out loud at such unanticipated, and blatant, display of jealousy. *"Not at all, Jiangsu tài. I just didn't want to disturb your official conferences."*

Zhao Jiangsu didn't answer as he was busy looking around his apartment. *"You know…"* the old man began, scratching his chin. *"This place looks different than it did before."*

Elias glanced around his flat although he already knew what was different. There was more light and more air in the place now that Elias had pushed aside the thick curtains which remained open at all times. There was no more room for darkness in his life. Elias smiled and said, *"I guess it's just your presence, Jiangsu tài."*

"Ha-ha!" the old man laughed, and his eyes turned into half-moons. He sat down on the sofa and asked Elias if he might offer his guest a drink like people usually did, even in these parts of the world.

Elias shook his head and said, *"My apologies, Jiangsu tài. I threw away all the alcohol I had in here. I didn't want the temptation around me."*

Zhao Jiangsu watched him with surprise on his face for a moment before he smiled proudly. *"It's just what I expected of you,"* he beamed. *"Is it very hard to give up alcohol?"*

Elias sighed as he sat down across Zhao Jiangsu. *"I will admit it is not easy. I had severe cravings for it for days after I stopped drinking. The meetings have helped me deal with that. They even referred me to a doctor who has been helping me get over this addiction, as he calls it."*

"I am so happy that you are building a healthy life for yourself, my child. It is nothing less than you deserve," the older man said.

"Speaking of which, I'll say my health has considerably improved because I've also begun writing music again," Elias shared. The old man was the second person after Fei who Elias had confided in about writing the piece that he was currently.

"Oh you are?" Zhao Jiangsu sat, sitting up straight.

"Yes," Elias said, pointing toward the small desk where he sat and wrote his music. It was right in front of the glass window, and looked drenched in warm sunlight.

"This is exciting," the old man said, rubbing his hands.

"Can I perhaps listen to a little of what you have written?"

Elias hesitated for a moment before he got up to his feet. Even after so many years, he was assailed by self-doubts for a few seconds. However, he knew how to stamp down on those feelings. He knew he was good; and he also understood that this might just be the best piece of music he had ever written. Besides, this was Jiangsu tài – Elias had played for him several times when he was young and he knew the old man would be good first audience for this piece of music.

Elias caught the music sheet in his hand and took his violin from its resting place on the shelf. Then he settled on the sofa in front of Zhao Jiangsu who quietly watched Elias prepare to play his music. Pulling his violin out of its case, Elias put it against his chin and closed his eyes as he began to play the melody from memory.

The sweet notes began to pour into the room. Zhao Jiangsu closed his eyes, too, as he began to savour the music that almost brought him to tears. It tugged at his heart – though it wasn't a sad song. It was a song of love. It made Zhao Jiangsu yearn for a lost love, and a lost lifetime: he suddenly missed his wife who had died several years ago, leaving him alone. The music spoke of love's bittersweet ache and its delight. Slowly, the music began to fade away till it completed vanished. Zhao Jiangsu opened his eyes and saw Elias looking at him expectantly. Elias saw that he didn't need the old man to give his review in words. He looked so moved that Elias got his answer.

Zhao Jiangsu sat motionless for a few moments. Then he cleared his throat before he said, *"That was...that was something else, Elias."*

Elias smiled in response. *"I am glad you like it."*

"I loved it. Do you know what it reminded me of?"

"What?"

"It reminded me of Azaleas in Bloom. Although that is a happier song than this one, I felt the same flood of love in this that I did in Hwang Yau-Tai's song when I first listened to it."

"Hwang Yau-Tai?" Elias's ears perked up at this name which was so familiar to him.

He knew the composer of course but just now when Zhao Jiangsu had said the name, it had reminded him of another memory entirely: that of sitting with his father and mother in the small musical hall of Tientsin, and listening to a very young composer play his piece on the stage. Suddenly, the present world vanished and he saw once again the most beautiful memory of his parents before his eyes. The music that had played then began to play in his mind again as he recollected how his father and mother had smiled at each other and held each other's hand.

"Oh..." Elias said, sitting up straight. He realised now where he had taken the inspiration to write this piece of music. Now that he knew love himself, his mind had unconsciously gone back to the first time he had understood the love that can exist between a man and a woman. Without knowing how, he had mined the memory and recreated it, although, as Zhao Jiangsu had said, in a different form. The inspiration source still lingered in his piece in that it conveyed the same emotions. Elias felt grateful, and a little bit overwhelmed. Life had offered to him more things than he had ever dared to ask of it, he felt.

Zhao Jiangsu said, *"One day, my son, I will ask you to play Azaleas in Bloom for me. I believe you are the only person who will do justice to it."*

Collecting himself, Elias smiled and said, *"You know, my father loved the music of Hwang Yau-Tai, too. I often played the pieces he composed for my father and mother, although the musician was not very well-known at the time. He came to visit Tientsin when we lived there, and that's when my parents fell in love with his talents."*

"I remember you playing one of his pieces for me and my family, too. That happened at the time that you lived with us in Yancheng, before you left for Hong Kong."

"Ah yes. Those were the days…" Elias reminisced. He thought back to the time that he had spent with Zhao Jiangsu's family in Yancheng. Though he was there for only a week before leaving for Hong Kong, and there was war and scarcity, that period was still rich in memories for him. He thought back to that time often, even before Zhao Jiangsu and Fei had reappeared in his life. It was the first time after his parents' deaths that he had felt happy and safe. That time, like all good times, had ended. He had moved on but he had those memories to cherish.

"I am still sorry you had to part with your beloved violin, my son," Zhao Jiangsu said with regret as he settled deeper into the sofa, and crossed his arms over his chest.

Elias waved his hand in the air as though asking the old man to not mention it. Yet the old man now seemed in the mood to reminisce. Elias didn't think it right to stop him from thinking back to the old times. He had understood that going over one's past often served as catharsis. He let the old man speak, and felt himself once more going back in time…

***

It was the morning after Zhao Jiangsu and Elias had arrived at the family home in Yancheng. After eating a scare breakfast of old buns and soymilk, Elias had gone outside with Fei while Zhao Jiangsu remained inside. He was not sure of how the townspeople – his own neighbours of several years – might interpret his presence here when he was supposed to be in the army.

He spent several agonising hours inside before he decided to venture out of the home. He was prepared to face the ostracism that he might have to; head-on. He walked outside and saw the old grandfather of his friend. The man was around a hundred years old or even older but he was still living.

"*Zhàng[12] Wu!*" Zhao Jiangsu called out. The old man, who was sitting idle outside his small house watching the children play in the streets, looked up at him.

"*Zhao Jiangsu!*" he said, wobbling to his feet. Zhao Jiangsu leapt toward him and caught his arm. In his old age, the man should have been walking with a walking cane but he didn't bother to; it apparently hurt his pride, like he had told Jiangsu so many years ago.

"*How are you?*" Zhao Jiangsu asked him.

Wu sighed and said, "*How can I be when all five of my grandsons, and three of my great-grandsons have been killed in the war? I did not want to outlive them.*"

Zhao Jiangsu patted the old man's shoulder. There were no words he could offer that would dilute the heartbreak of losing your sons in your lifetime. The old man never asked him what he was doing here, or why he wasn't in the army. It appeared that he was beyond such questions now, and wanted to pass no moral judgment on anyone. In fact, he told Zhao Jiangsu to protect his family for the war had not abated.

---

[12] A prefix used to address elderly people.

The two men got talking about all that Zhao Jiangsu had seen in the war. He was the only man that Jiangsu had confided to at this time of his life. When they ran out of words, they sat side by side in comfortable silence and watched the kids run here and there. This was their game – to chase each other. The old man remarked how the kids' childhood in this country had been ruined and Zhao Jiangsu couldn't help but agree.

He felt a pang of sorrow as he looked at Elias who was laughing freely for the first time since his parents had died. Even at the hospital as he had recovered he had merely smiled sometimes – a timid, fearful smile that vanished before it could reach his eyes; but now, he was laughing as any carefree child should. He told Wu about Elias's tragic fate – how his parents had been killed and how he had become an orphan and the old man shook his head at the little child's loss.

"I hope he recovers. I hope he makes his parents proud," Wu said.

"I think he will," Zhao Jiangsu said, nodding his head with a certainty he didn't know the source of.

***

"Did the old man survive the war?" Elias asked as Zhao Jiangsu finished telling him the story.

"No. Unfortunately, he wasn't alive when I was finally able to come back to my hometown with Fei and Ling. His granddaughter told me he had passed away in his sleep."

"I hope he rests in peace," Elias said.

"You know what I learned from this old man?" Zhao Jiangsu asked.

"What?"

"When I was younger, before the war had begun and upended our lives, this old man taught me to meditate. I learned from him to channel inner peace. He taught me how to sit and meditate so that the worries of this world fall from me, like leaves fall off a tree in autumn. The process of acceptance – of what has happened and what will come to happen – is as natural as that."

Elias listened quietly. In truth, his mind could not fathom peace of that magnitude. Though bad things had happened in his life, at some level he had never let them pass through him – in other words, he had never accepted them. His pain was still like a tightly-curled fist inside his chest. He was trying to open that fist now, and to let go, but the process was long and excruciating.

"How can I do the same?" he asked.

"You, too, should practise meditation, my son," Zhao Jiangsu answered. *"Read about it, and I will tell you, as well. I will teach you what Old Wu taught me. I know it will help you regain your balance in life."*

"I will do that," Elias said, thinking about it. The idea appealed to him.

Zhao Jiangsu shuffled to his feet. *"I should be getting back. I phoned Fei and asked her to wait up for dinner."*

"Let me walk you to the car," Elias offered as he helped the old man into his coat.

Chapter 15
Season of Migration

"But how are you so good at it?" Fei Hong, a boy Elias's age, asked. He sounded more bewildered than amazed at Elias's musical skills.

"I just am!" Elias explained, for the umpteenth time. His new friends in Yancheng, where he had arrived a few days ago, had made it a routine to gather around Elias for music sessions every morning. Sometimes they listened to his music quietly, other times they tried to dance to it; they also told their parents and extended family about it, impressed as they were with Elias's talent.

In a matter of a few days, Elias had become a little celebrity. Even the adults sometimes gathered to listen to him play. One of the frequent attendees was a middle-aged, crippled man Qing Shan who had not joined the war because of his disability. He told Elias he had attended many musical concerts before the war – in fact, he wanted to be a piano player himself but could not train because he couldn't enrol at the institute which was in the central city of Beijing.

So, he told Elias, *"I settled for collecting whatever musical instruments I could get my hands on!"*

He had invited Elias for a tour of his home and Elias was surprised to see that he had all sorts of musical instruments in his house – it was rather like a museum of music. Qing Shan said, *"I have seen your violin, Elias, and am pleased to say it is of fine quality. It looks very old to me, but someone has obviously looked after it well."*

Elias had said, *"It was my father's. He brought it here with him from Russia."*

"Oh, Russia," Qing Shan said, impressed. Then he cleared his throat and added, *"If you ever want to sell it, I would love to buy it. I will pay you a good amount for it."*

Elias had recoiled at the offer. He had not liked the proposition at all. It was the only thing of his father's that he possessed and he would never part with it!

Other than the unwelcome offer, Elias didn't mind things here at Yancheng. For the first time since his parents had died, he felt like he belonged. His friends made him feel right at home. It was another thing entirely that he knew he would have to depart from this city soon as Zhao Jiangsu had planned.

"Can you teach me, too?" Zhi Ruo, a little girl of about five years of age, asked. She treated Elias like a hero. She looked at him with wide worshipping eyes and tagged along with him all day. Elias, who'd never had a sibling, had begun to love her like one.

"Yes, I will teach you, Zhi Ruo!" he smiled at the little girl and then ruffled her hair. She scrunched up her nose, smiled, and sat back down beside her older sister. After playing another piece, Elias excused himself and walked home – that is, Zhao Jiangsu's home. It wasn't his home, but he had started to feel like it was. Fei and her mother, whose animosity he had feared, made him feel like a part of their family. Ling, Zhao Jiangsu's wife, fussed over him and made sure he ate on time, just like his mother.

On his short walk home, Elias thought what he could do to make things somewhat better for the family. It hadn't escaped Elias's notice that the food supplies, even since the night that he had come here, had started to dwindle. He had watched Ling cut down on her food portions; lately, she had come down to eating just one meal during the day. Elias couldn't help but feel guilty.

After all, he was one extra mouth to feed for the family. They never complained or made him feel like he was imposing, but Elias felt responsible nevertheless.

"I am home!" he announced as he stepped inside the small house.

"Elias, child, you are late. I made some vegetable soup, and it's almost cold now. Do you want it?" Ling said, emerging from the kitchen area.

Fei was sitting on the floor, practising her handwriting. She ignored the exchange between her mother and Elias. After having introduced him to her other friends, Fei now sometimes left him alone with them. He was getting along with them just fine, and she felt a little proud of him for fitting right in though he had been here for only a few days.

Elias nodded. At his age, he had quite an appetite. The food that he got was never enough for him, but that was the way of wars – short on peace, short on supplies. A minute later, Ling came out of the kitchen carrying a small bowl. She set it in front of Elias and instructed him to eat slowly. Elias nodded, but he had no intention of doing what she'd said.

He was ravenous, and in this state, he couldn't help but wolf down his food. He had no patience for savouring the taste anymore. He dipped the spoon into the bowl and swallowed the first mouthful. It was lukewarm and watery, more broth than soup. Elias didn't mind though – as long as he had something that would fill him up for a while.

Watching him eat, Fei rolled her eyes. Ling sat down in front of him and shook her head. *"It is useless to teach you table manners, boy,"* she said to Elias who grinned in response. He knew she wasn't unkind; she only wanted to drill some etiquettes into him, as his mother had done.

Ling sighed and said, *"I wonder where Zhao Jiangsu Jiangsu went. He hasn't been back since dawn."*

Fei said, *"Probably he went to make the arrangements to leave. Remember, he said we leave in two days?"*

"Ah yes," Ling said. She didn't bother to express her regrets or fears at leaving her hometown for a strange land. You had to do what you had to do; complaining never had and never would change the facts. Besides, she knew it was for their own safety that her husband had taken this decision. The whole day passed, and it was around midnight that Zhao

Jiangsu returned.

Taking off his coat, he told Ling, *"We leave tomorrow night. Yancheng will not be safe from the Japanese for very long. If we miss the junk this time, I don't know when it will transport people to a safe place again."*

Elias and Fei exchanged a glance. The two of them kept quiet and did not interrupt the adults' discussion; however, they wanted to be aware of their immediate fate, so they listened intently.

Ling asked, *"So what do we carry with us?"*

"Only the clothes on your back. Maybe one sack of spare clothing. I am afraid the junk will already have more people than it can possibly hold," Zhao Jiangsu said. Then he cleared his throat and added, *"The only problem is...."*

"What?" Ling asked.

"It's just they charge an exorbitant amount for smuggling people out of the country. I fear that we may not have enough money. I have sold some things today and have a good sum, but I just don't know what they might demand."

"Is it too much?" Ling asked with a concerned frown on her face.

Zhao Jiangsu said, *"I really don't know for sure, but I think so. I am a little afraid."*

"What can we do about it, Zhao Jiangsu? We will cross that bridge when we come to it," Ling said resignedly. *"We will ask them to show compassion. I am sure they will take the money we do have and let us on the junk."*

Elias heard the entire exchange. He instantly knew there was only one way out – just one way that he could help this generous, hospitable family. He didn't say anything, though, and went to sleep with the idea rankling in his head. The next day was their last in Yancheng. Elias and Fei had the instructions to behave like it was any other day. Zhao Jiangsu told them not to say goodbye to any of their friends.

They had to pretend that they would be here tomorrow when in fact by then they would be on their way to Hong Kong. Elias spent the day with his friends that he had been with for far too little time. He already loved them all, especially Zhi Ruo. It was almost dusk and their play-time was about to end. Elias played his violin for his friends one last time and smiled. The others cheered for him like they always did and started to head home. As Zhi Ruo was leaving, Elias caught up to her and bent down to her height. Then he ruffled her hair and said, *"Be good, Zhi Ruo."* Turning to his older sister, Elias said, *"Take care of her."* Both of them nodded obediently and walked away without looking back.

Fei, who was with him this evening, put her hand on his shoulder and said, *"You are going to miss her, right?"*

Elias said, *"Yes. I hope she stays safe. One day when the war is over, I will come back and teach her how to play the violin."*

Fei's smile turned into a puzzled frown when Elias began to walk in the opposite direction of home. *"Where are you going?"* she called out to him.

"You go on home. I'll be back in a little while. Tell your mother not to worry, I'll be right there," Elias called out and ran off before Fei could ask any more questions.

Elias knew where he had to go and he walked fast, lest his heart changed. Reaching the house he had visited a few days ago, he rapped on the door. A few minutes passed, but no one answered the knock. Growing impatient, Elias knocked again. A yell emerged from within, *"Coming! I am coming! Would you show patience to a crippled man?"* Elias regretted the second knock instantly. He knew Qing Shan had no wife or kids; his mother, who took care of him, had passed on a few years ago and the man now lived alone. The door opened, and Elias saw the man he was looking for leaning heavily against a makeshift walking stick.

Qing Shan's eyebrows rose in surprise when he saw Elias. *"What are you doing here, kid?"* he asked bluntly.

"I came here to take you up on your offer," Elias answered.

If it were possible, Qing Shan's eyebrows rose up even more. *"Come on in then,"* he said, making way for Elias to enter the house.

After that, it took only a few minutes of haggling for the price before the deal was closed. Elias had sold his father's violin for money – but this money would ensure the protection of the people to whom he owed his life.

***

Elias walked inside Zhao Jiangsu's house and handed him the money without saying a word. Ling and Fei watched the proceedings but did not speak.

"Where did you get it?" Zhao Jiangsu asked, surprise evident on his face.

"I sold my violin."

"You what?" Ling said, horrified.

"But it was your father's, Elias! And you said you loved it!" Fei cried.

Elias nodded and said, *"But Jiangsu tài said we needed money for the junk. So I sold it."*

"I will not accept this!" Zhao Jiangsu protested. *"I will get the violin back right now. We know how much it meant to you, Elias."*

Elias shook his head and said, *"If you return the money then I will run away. I won't go to Hong Kong with you!"*

"Elias!" Ling exclaimed, *"Why are you saying such things? We are your family, and you will come with us!"*

Elias stood his ground. *"If you truly think I am a part of your family then you will accept the money. I did it to keep all of us safe as I would do for my parents."*

Tears came into Zhao Jiangsu's eyes at Elias's show of big-heartedness. He knew they needed the money and that it could not be arranged from any other source at such short notice. While he hated that Elias had to sell his violin, he knew there was no other option.

"I will remember your kindness, child," Ling said.

Elias only smiled. He did not tell her that he felt no matter what he did for Zhao Jiangsu and his family, he could never pay back for what they had done for him. The next few hours passed in a blur. There was news of imminent, unexpected airstrike on the city's borders. Zhao Jiangsu knew the strategy of the Japanese army well.

He knew if there were airstrikes, the ports would definitely come under attack. They had to leave sooner than they had expected. Taking the one rucksack which contained a set of spare clothes and a few belongings with them, the family of three and Elias stepped out of the home and started to walk to the port. They had almost reached the docks when the bombing began. It happened far off to the west, but the fighter planes were approaching fast in their direction.

"The junk might leave earlier than its time now. Hurry, hurry!" Zhao Jiangsu said, picking up speed.

The four of them were almost jogging now. The night sky, it seemed, was ripped open in one place as bombs were dropped. Fire came raining down. The four of them couldn't hear anything above the roar and kept running. Elias found it hard to breathe. The sight of fire took him back to the night --- the horrible night when there were small fires on the streets, and his parents were snatched away from him. Pangs of loss racked him, and he felt tears running down his cheeks. He saw as the distance between him and the family of three increased. He heard as the planes got closer, and there was a deafening roar of a blast nearby.

Elias collapsed to his knees, panting for breath. He could not go on, he did not want to go on.

He felt the heat of the blast at his back. In the awful smoke, he could see nothing. He rubbed his sore eyes and stared at the figure that appeared out of the smog, like an angel that no one but he could see. It was running towards him at top speed. Wiping his face with his hands, he recognised who it was: Fei. She had come running back to get him. Even in the state of utter despair and panic, he knew what Fei's actions meant. She had put her own life in danger to rescue him. Fei caught Elias's arms and ignoring his mumbling, pulled him to his feet. Then she took off, and Elias had no choice but to run with her.

Emerging through the dense cloud of smoke, Elias saw the figures of Zhao Jiangsu and Ling waiting for them a few metres ahead. Fei ran to them, and when they were together, Zhao Jiangsu directed them to keep running to the left. They took a short alley, and there was the port in front of them. The air was humid and smelled clean, though a bit salty. Elias felt the wind push his hair back as they got to the harbour.

In the dim lights, Elias saw the junk waiting. It was already full of people who seemed to be jostling each other for space. A man was standing to the side, urgently motioning them to hurry up.

"This is my family. I talked to you about them," Zhao Jiangsu reminded the man.

"Yes, yes, I know," the man said irritably. *"You are late. I was about to leave without you. Now, did you bring the money for three people?"*

Fei and Elias looked at each other. Three people?

"Yes, I did. Here is the money," Zhao Jiangsu said, ignoring the gazes of the two kids and his wife on him. He ruffled through his pocket and pulled out the money. As they had decided before leaving, Zhao Jiangsu offered half the money they had.

The smuggler quickly counted the money and shook his head. *"With this much money, I will take only two people."*

"But these were your rates!" Zhao Jiangsu protested.

"That was before the air raid," the man said, turning away. *"I don't have time to waste here. If you can't pay up, step aside. We leave in five minutes."*

Zhao Jiangsu reluctantly offered some more money. He said, *"This is all I have. It is enough for my wife and the two kids."*

The man snatched the money and counted it down to the last note. Then, looking at them as if he was conferring the biggest favour and hadn't just exhorted a considerable sum from them, he nodded curtly. *"Get in. Two minutes to say your goodbyes,"* he spat.

As the man walked to the side, Zhao Jiangsu said, *"I am not going with you."*

Ling clutched her husband's arm and pleaded, *"Come with us. We have some money left. What are you going to do here, Zhao Jiangsu?"*

He patted Ling's hand and gently extracted his arm out of her grasp. *"I have to rejoin the army, Ling. I am a soldier, and I have a duty to my country. You take care of the two kids, now. Go on, get on the junk. You will be just fine."*

Zhao Jiangsu turned to Elias and Fei and said, *"Don't worry her, you two. I will see you soon."* He hugged all three of them and then ushered them over the wobbly plank and into the junk.

The man got in, and the junk started to sail. Ling stood between Elias and Fei, holding their hands. Tears slipped down her face, and she didn't care to wipe them away. The two children waved to Zhao Jiangsu, and he waved back. They kept waving till his figure receded in the darkness of the night, and they could see him no more.

***

Getting to Hong Kong was easier than settling down in the city. It was a small place, bursting at the seams with people of various colours and languages. Ling had some of the money that Zhao Jiangsu had handed to her as she had stepped into the junk. With that money, she secured quarters and some food for her small family. The money, all of them knew, would not last long. They had to find a way to survive, and soon.

In the next few days, it became apparent that they would have to live off the charity of international aid organisations that operated in Hong Kong. There were no jobs to be had, no were there any other sources to earn money.

Elias spent his days with Fei. They played in the streets and attended informal classes that a charity organisation had arranged for refugee children. Ling had made friends with other refugee women. They knitted sweaters for an aid group and were paid a pittance for it. Ling was grateful for that, however; something was better than nothing.

Almost to the year after they had got to Hong Kong, Ling was able to secure a job as a cook in the kitchen at the British military base. The former cook had departed for America, leaving the coveted post empty. One of the workers in the aid organisation referred me to Ling, and she got the position. The pay was not good, but it was more than they'd had for the entire years they had been in Hong Kong. They could afford to buy some food with it but little else.

There were days that Elias missed his violin. He missed his parents, and he also missed Zhao Jiangsu. He hoped in his heart that the man who had been a father to him would survive the war. They had not heard from Zhao Jiangsu – and how would they? He did not know their address, and they did not know which part of China he was in. Ling patiently waited for the war to be over as she believed that's when she would make contact with her husband again.

One evening, when Elias and Fei came back from the class, Ling was already home. She had made cabbage soup and told them to wash up so she could serve dinner.

During dinner, Elias and Fei both noticed that Ling was distracted. She hardly ate her soup and stared off into space with a frown on her face. By now, Elias had learned to communicate with Fei without saying a word. They had conveyed their concerns about Ling to each other already, by glancing and quirking their eyebrows at each other every now and then. Now it was up to one of them to ask her what was up. Elias lifted his brow to give Fei the get-go: she would be the one to enquire of her mother about what was on her mind.

"Mother, may I ask, why are you so worried?" Fei said politely.

"Eh?" Ling said, looking disoriented.

Fei repeated, *"Why are you worried, Mother?"*

"I am not worried. I have just heard news. A...good news," Ling said. There was indecision on her face as if she could not decide whether to tell them or not. Then she made up her mind and spoke: *"I have been talking to an officer at the military base. He knows people at the American embassy."*

"American?" Fei repeated and looked at Elias who shrugged. He had no idea what America had to do with anything.

"Yes. You kids know that another World War has started, correct?"

"Yes, Miss Heaney told us at school," Elias said.

"Well, ever since then, America has opened its doors for

people who are hunted by Hitler," Ling said.

Again, Fei and Elias looked at each other. They just couldn't see where this conversation was heading. Hitler was killing people, but that was far away in Europe. In geography lessons, they had learned they lived in Asia which was at a considerable distance from Hitler. Moreover, America was even farther away. So they did not know where Ling was going with all the talk of America and Hitler, who were none of their concern.

"What are you saying, Mother?" Fei decided to ask openly. Her patience had already run out. She wanted to know the story quickly so she could go and work on her homework for the drawing lessons. She had to draw her childhood home which she remembered and missed dearly.

"The American Embassy here will send people of the Jewish faith to live in America. It will be a safer, more prosperous life there for the Jews."

"Jews?" Fei said, even more impatiently than before. She turned to look at Elias, but this time, he was not looking at her. He was staring at Ling. It seemed like he understood what her mother was saying while Fei was still unable to

connect the dots. She watched Elias's face for a few moments and then unconsciously straightened in her chair. The expressions on Elias's face were grave. Her mother, too, was looking at Elias. There seemed to be an unspoken conversation going on between them.

"What is it? What is it?" Fei said.

Ling turned to look at her impatient daughter and sighed. *"Elias will be better off living in America."*

"What?" Fei gasped. The thought of sending her friend so far away – America was the other side of the world practically! – was unfathomable to her. It was impossible. She would never allow it!

"Elias won't go!" Fei declared. She looked at her friend for his approval, but he did not say a word. He seemed lost in thought.

"Hong Kong is not safe from the Japanese. The officers at the camp expect Japan to attack soon – if not this year then the next. The safest bet for people is to move as far away from the Japanese army as possible," Ling explained. *"I am more worried for Elias because he is Jewish. The world is not kind to Jews, not in these times. This is why I want him*

to travel to America and make a life for himself there."

"But how will Elias go without us, Mother? We can't send him so far away all alone!" Fei protested.

"What is to be done must be done," Ling said plainly. From her manner, she seemed to have decided to pursue the matter, and to send off Elias to America. *"I have already talked to the officer who told me about the process. This morning, I went to the embassy to get all the details. I think it will take three to four weeks at the maximum for Elias to be processed before he will depart for New York."*

"Mother!" Fei objected again.

Ling stood from the floor with the soup bowls in her hand. She said to her daughter, *"Think of what is best for Elias, not for yourself. He is not safe here. He must go."* She went outside the house to wash the bowl with the water in the pail that she kept outside the door.

Fei turned to Elias with tears in her eyes. *"Will you go?"* she pleaded, desperately hoping he would put his foot down and refuse to leave.

Elias, on the other hand, was thinking not of his safety but the convenience of this small family. He knew if Ling had one less mouth to feed, things would become much more comfortable for her money-wise. She wouldn't have to work double shifts and would be able to stay home on Sundays. She might even be able to afford warm clothes for herself and Fei.

"I will go," Elias confirmed. He ignored the tears in Fei's eyes though it hurt his heart to see his dear friend cry. *"I have to go,"* he repeated to leave no doubt in Fei's mind that he, too, had made his decision.

The next few days passed in a flurry of activity. Fei went to her classes alone, sulking every morning, as Elias went with Ling to the American embassy. She had to take leaves of absence from her job at the base, but she did it for Elias; he appreciated her selflessness though he did worry about the loss of income her absences would mean.

The process was quicker than Ling had anticipated. America seemed to be in a frenzy to save people for some reason – especially the children. Instead of three or four weeks, it took only two. Elias was set to leave for America fifteen days after Ling had broken the news to them. On the day of his departure, he hugged Ling and thanked her for her kindness to him. He also told her that he would visit her after the war, and asked her to send Zhao Jiangsu his warm regards. To Fei, he said nothing because she was very busy crying. He only shook her hand and gave her a brief hug. Both mother and daughter came to see him off at the tarmac. He got on the plane and waved goodbye. He did not know then that he would never see Ling, who was like a mother to him, ever again. He did not know then that ages would pass before he would be reunited with Fei, the old friend that his heart never forgot.

Chapter 16
The Final Goodbye

"Did you ever try to contact us again, Elias?" Fei asked as she dug into her lasagna.

Fei was at Elias's place, and they were having a quiet, private dinner. Almost a year had passed since Fei had come from China and over six months since she had started dating Elias. She could safely say that this was the happiest year of her life. In Elias, she had found a mate who not only understood her but who drove her to be a better version of herself. She knew she did the same for him.

Perhaps it was their bond forged in childhood, but Fei felt she knew Elias better than he knew himself.

Elias swallowed his mouthful and said, *"I did actually."*

Fei quirked her eyebrows in surprise and question. She curled her hand around the wine glass, and said, *"Really? I thought you wanted to leave the past in the past. We never received a letter or a call…"*

"*I contacted the military base in Hong Kong where your mother used to work,*" Elias said. "*This was after the war had ended. Before that, the authorities never let the calls through to conflict-ridden areas.*"

"*Then? Didn't they tell you where she was?*"

"*They confirmed that they had one Zhao Ling in their employ until recently, but she had departed for her home country a few months previously. And that she had not left a forwarding address.*"

"*Oh. You must have called after Father had come to Hong Kong to get us. He came to get us as soon as the war ended in 1945. We barely had two days to wrap everything up and leave for Yancheng again.*"

Elias said, "*There was no way for me to establish contact in Yancheng. The diplomatic channels between the USA and China were pretty much non-existent at the time. Plus, China had just been through a massive war and was in complete disarray. The government, the infrastructure, everything was in ruins. I was told I wouldn't be able to contact anybody in China unless I travelled to the country.*"

Understanding dawned in Fei's eyes. *"Ah, it makes sense. You could hardly travel to China during that time, what with the communist threat."*

"Correct," Elias said, sipping at his soda. It was no coincidence that he had a soft drink to go with his meal while Fei had wine. Elias had got his addictions under control in the time that had passed. And now, to be on the safe side, he kept away from alcohol altogether.

"Mother always spoke of you fondly till the time that she passed away. You were like a son to her," Fei smiled.

"And she was like a mother to me," Elias smiled back. *"I am so sorry that I never got to see her again. But I am glad I got to see you and Jiangsu tài."*

"Me too," Fei whispered as she bent towards Elias and kissed him.

Forgetting the dinner that was going cold, Elias wrapped his arms around Fei and kissed her back. Pausing, he took her face in his hands and said, *"Fei, I had to ask you for something."*

"Really, what?" Fei murmured.

"Your hand," Elias said.

"My hand?" Fei repeated, looking clueless. She lifted her hand, stared at it confusedly and handed it to Elias who began to laugh uproariously till tears streamed down his face.

Fei asked him a few times what was so funny, but that seemed to send him into fresh fits of laughter. Offended, Fei crossed her arms and waited in stony silence for her boyfriend to collect himself. That's how she treated both her father and Elias when they got it in their minds to mock her. Her condescending behaviour toward them hardly ever had an effect, but it was still better than protesting.

Finally, Elias wiped his face with his sleeve and clonked Fei on her head. He said, *"I am amazed that someone as smart as you can mistake my intentions."*

"Well, what are your intentions?" Fei demanded.

"Honest ones. I am asking for your hand. You know, in marriage?" Elias grinned.

"Oh!" Fei said, her eyes widening. *"Oh,"* she repeated as she absorbed Elias's words.

"Oh, indeed," Elias said, getting up from his place on the sofa.

He pulled Fei, who still looked shocked, to her feet. Then as she watched, Elias bent down on one knee before her and said, *"Fei, will you marry me?"*

Tears came into Fei's eyes. She couldn't speak though she tried to. Swallowing the lump in her throat, she nodded.

"Come on, say yes! I have to know for sure. I am too old to be on my knees for so long!" Elias joked.

Fei laughed through her tears and said, *"Yes. Yes, I will marry you!"* She tugged at Elias's hands, and he got to his feet. Standing before her, he smiled blissfully, as if he had come into possession of the world and all its treasures.

Dropping Fei's hands, he extracted a box from the pocket of his jeans. He opened the box to reveal a glittering diamond ring. It had a brilliant round cut, and as Elias put it on Fei's finger, she felt like it was made for her.

"Thank you for saying yes," Elias whispered as he kissed his fiancée's forehead.

"*You're welcome,*" Fei answered, resting her face in the crook of Elias's neck.

"*We have to tell Jiangsu tài,*" Elias said, wrapping his arms around Fei. "*Now I am wondering if I should have asked him first. For your hand in marriage, I mean…*"

Fei snorted. "*No, I am not that old-fashioned, Elias, despite what you think. Besides, you already have his approval.*"

Elias laughed, "*Yes, I do. We'll tell him together, then?*"

"*Yes, that would be best. I do want to see his reaction. For the past ten years, he has been telling me I run off men and that at this rate, I would die an old maid. Now I will prove him wrong!*"

Elias laughed and said, "*All right then. I will invite him out to lunch, and we will break the news to him.*"

"*Yes, he'll be back from China the day after tomorrow. Let's plan the lunch for Sunday,*" Fei said. Her father had been in his home country for the past week; he had said it was some official trip, and that he would be back in Washington after taking care of a few official matters.

"Jiangsu tài is working too much for a man his age. When he comes back, we will force him to take some rest. He has had such a busy year!"

Fei sighed. *"You try and tell him to rest, Elias. He never listens to me."*

Elias nodded and said, *"I will! Half his health will improve when we tell him our news."*

"He'll be over the moon!" Fei grinned. *"He'll probably be happier than you."*

"Wrong," Elias contradicted with a smile of contentment. *"No one can be happier than I am in this moment."*

***

Zhao Jiangsu had not been feeling well lately. He felt more tired than usual, and his appetite had gone down drastically. He had taken care not to tell his daughter or Elias, however; they were so happy lately that he did not want to spoil it by worrying them.

And this afternoon, they had invited him for lunch. He had a hunch they were going to surprise him with good news. Owing to his declining health, Zhao Jiangsu was also thinking of retiring from his post. He was too old and too exhausted now to continue and do a good job. He also missed his homeland. But before he went back, he wanted to spend some more time with Elias. If he left, who knew if he would see Elias ever again?

Zhao Jiangsu also had a few things to care of before he retired and retreated into a quiet life. He had some things in his possession that he had to return to their owner. For years, he had it in his safekeeping, not knowing if life would ever give him the chance to restore it to whom it belonged. Now it was time to give it back.

It was Elias's old violin – the one that was his father's, and that he had sold to ensure the safety of Zhao Jiangsu's family.

Once the war had ended, Zhao Jiangsu had made his way to Hong Kong. He had collected his family from the city and travelled back to his hometown of Yancheng. Setting foot in the city had felt like a dream to him; he had not expected to survive the war and be back home again. It was an uphill task from there to rebuild his life, but he had done it with his wife Ling by his side. In all this, he never forgot the little boy who had taught him a thing or two about resilience and kindness.

Soon after coming back home, he had managed to trace the violin. He knew in his neighbourhood, there was no one but Qing Shan who would have bought the violin from Elias. It wasn't exactly easy for Zhao Jiangsu to get the violin back from Qing Shan who had refused to part with it; in his estimation, the old violin, with its beautiful case, was a rare jewel seldom found so well-preserved and at such reasonable price too. But Zhao Jiangsu had his ways. It involved a lot of money changing hands, but the cost was a small matter for Zhao Jiangsu who knew the real value of the instrument.

He had kept the violin with him for all these years. He was not sure if he would ever see Elias again. He held it in hopes that he would. Just a week ago, he had travelled back to Yancheng. He'd furnished a good excuse for Fei and Elias, one that would stop them for detaining him in America. He had said that he was heading back to China for an official meeting. In truth, he had gone back only to collect the violin. The travel back and forth had drained him, but the trip was well worth the joy he knew it would bring to Elias. It was time to hand it back. Once he was back in Washington, Elias had promptly asked him out on lunch. It was just as well.

He had told Elias to pick him up from his apartment that he shared with his daughter. Elias arrived before time. He seemed to be in a hurry, walking fast and talking fast. Zhao Jiangsu told him to sit down and wait.

"But we are running late!" Elias claimed.

"We are not. You got here early if anything. Anyway, they won't give our table away, I am sure of that," Zhao Jiangsu said, forcing Elias to take a seat. Then without listening to further protests, he walked inside his bedroom and closed the door.

Outside, Fei crossed her legs and hid her smile. Her fiancé was tapping his fingers against the armrest, in time to some tune she could not hear; it was a sure sign of impatience, maybe even nervousness.

"Are you nervous?" Fei finally asked, biting down her lower lip to keep herself from laughing.

"No," Elias refused flatly. Then he hesitated before confessing, *"Well, a little, you can say. What if your father refuses?"*

Fei laughed this time. When Elias stared at her sullenly, she said, *"He is more your father than mine by now, Elias!*

So even if he does refuse, it will be because he doesn't approve of me as a wife for you rather than the other way round."

Elias rolled his eyes and opened his mouth to speak. The arrival of Zhao Jiangsu, however, cut him off before he began.

The old man was hefting a violin case. It took Elias only a few moments to recognise what it was. He sat dumbstruck. He was unable to speak or move, though somewhere in his mind it registered that he should get up and help Zhao Jiangsu who was panting from the effort of hauling the large box.

Putting the case on the coffee table before Elias, Zhao Jiangsu said, *"Here it is, Elias. Your violin returned to you in good shape."*

Elias looked at the violin case, then at Zhao Jiangsu and then back at the violin. He could not believe his eyes.

"My violin?" Elias rasped.

Zhao Jiangsu smiled and spread his arms as if to welcome him in a big hug. *"Yours."*

Fei sat silent and still, watching the emotional scene unfold before her. She, of course, knew that her father had reclaimed Elias's old violin from Qing Shan as soon as he had got back to Yancheng after the war. After the night that he had brought the violin back home, and told Ling he would make sure to give it back to Elias one day before he died, Fei had never seen it again.

She had presumed her father had hidden it in one of his safety chests, the ones that only he had the keys to. She had forgotten all about the old violin until this moment. And now, the memories of that fateful night when Elias had shown his generous heart to her, came rushing back. She couldn't help but feel proud of the man she had committed herself to for life.

Elias reached toward the violin case but did not pick it up. He traced his fingertips over the smooth surface, feeling the inedible print of his personal history on it. He felt as if the case was pulsating with life – that it was a living, breathing thing that knew Elias's history, his griefs, and his triumphs. His father's hands had touched this violin was the one thought that ran through Elias's head. It was a storehouse of memories – irreplaceable, and priceless.

Picking it up, Elias ran his hands down the case and opened it. He took his very first violin out and caressed it as if it were an old lover he had been reunited with after long years.

"Thank you, Jiangsu tài. I don't know what to say," Elias said in a hoarse voice as he blinked back tears.

The old man smiled and said, *"You don't have to say anything. I understand."* Then he added, *"But you have to play something for me."*

Elias laughed and said, *"Anything you want, Jiangsu tài."*

Zhao Jiangsu perked up. *"In that case, play me Hwang Yau-Tai's Azaleas in Bloom."*

Elias smiled and got ready to play.

Fei commented, *"Hwang Yau-Tai wrote 'Azaleas' in 1941, do you both know? In the middle of a war, he created a thing of beauty."*

Elias nodded and motioned Fei to come to sit beside him. Once she was seated, he started to play. The sweet notes spilt into the room, and Zhao Jiangsu closed his eyes in appreciation. Fei gave a smile of delight and stared straight into Elias's eyes as he continued to play with the mastery he was known for all over the world. As the song rose in a crescendo, Elias looked into her eyes and pledged his life to her, much like his mother and father had on the day buried beneath the dust of time but alive always in Elias's heart.

***

Fei and Elias got married in a discreet ceremony. The only guest was Zhao Jiangsu who cried like a mother on the auspicious day.

"Now you have made me happy beyond anything, children," he said as he patted the heads of his daughter and new son-in-law, congratulating them on their marriage.

The two of them smiled at him and dragged him off to lunch, the one that they had missed the other day because they had got so caught up in playing music and reminiscing. Elias and Fei had told the old man their decision at the apartment, and he was, as expected, overjoyed.

"Fei is a lucky woman," Zhao Jiangsu had said.

Fei gave Elias an I-told-you-so look as Elias laughed and countered, *"I am the one that is lucky, Jiangsu tài."*

For the first time in several months, Elias had had a glass of celebratory wine that afternoon. He was no longer afraid of being haunted by his demons, and of sliding back into his self-destructive way. He had become stronger, and happier. Now, he valued his life too much to go down the devastating spiral of addiction. Fei and Zhao Jiangsu had helped him come a long way from where he was only a year ago. If he looked back on his life, this was the time that things that had gone wrong for so long were set right again. He couldn't be more thankful than he was.

***

"Life has come full circle for us," Zhao Jiangsu said, holding Fei's hands but looking at Elias, telling him with his eyes to take care of his daughter when he was gone.

They were in China, the first home that Elias had ever known. This time, he had come back but only to say goodbye. Zhao Jiangsu, the man who was his father in all the way that meant something was dying, and Elias and Fei were by his side to send him off on his final journey. The old man was near death now. He was in the hospital, and the doctors had told them there was nothing they could do any more to help him.

His health had steadily deteriorated after Elias's and Fei's wedding. He had acted all bright and active till that time, but a couple of weeks after his daughter and son-in-law got back from their honeymoon, he had collapsed. The newly wedded couple had rushed him to the best hospital in Washington where the medical team told them it was old age that had got to Mr. Zhao and not a disease that they could cure.

Zhao Jiangsu had told Fei and Elias that he wanted to be back in his motherland to live out his last days in peace. Reluctantly, they had agreed. Elias had wanted to pursue further treatment, but he had to give up the idea since the old man was adamant about returning to China. He was convinced his end was near.

Fei sniffed and wiped away her tears with her free hand. Elias put his arm around his wife, and with the other, he held Zhao Jiangsu's hand.

The old man smiled at both of them and said, *"You two have each other. I can rest easy now."* He closed his eyes and breathed his last. Elias hugged Fei as she cried her heart out. He couldn't stop tears from flowing down his cheeks, for that matter. The two of them held each other as Zhao Jiangsu was laid to rest in his home city of Yancheng, alongside his ancestors and his beloved wife. Zhao Jiangsu was a good man – a strong and kind man who dared to confront his flaws and to right his wrongs. Elias realised that not many could claim that quality for themselves. For him, Zhao Jiangsu was a hero who had lived a remarkable life. He knew he would tell any children that he may have about their brave grandfather, who had taught their father and their mother how to live life with daring and how to reach for happiness that could be theirs, only if they showed a bit of courage and determination.

As Elias and Fei departed for Washington which they had made their home, they smiled at each other even though their hearts were sad. As Zhao Jiangsu had said, they had each other. Through thick and thin, and through good times and bad, the two of them had promised to be together. And that, Elias thought as he stepped inside the plane with his wife's hand tightly held in his, was the biggest blessing that he had received in his life.

10,000 GALLOPING HORSES

Printed in Poland
by Amazon Fulfillment
Poland Sp. z o.o., Wrocław